A MILLION WAYS HOME

A MILLION WAYS HOME

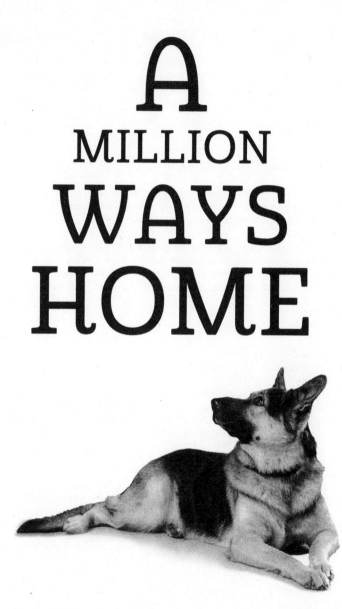

DIANNA DORISI WINGET

SCHOLASTIC PRESS | NEW YORK

Library of Congress Cataloging-in-Publication Data

Dorisi-Winget, Dianna, author.
 A million ways home / Dianna Dorisi Winget. — First edition.
  pages cm
 Summary: When her grandmother and guardian suffers a stroke, twelve-year-old
Poppy Parker's life turns upside down — but when she witnesses a murder and has to go
into witness protection with Detective Brannigan's mother it becomes hard to believe
she will ever find a way home, let alone save Gunner, a beautiful German shepherd with
an uncertain future.
 ISBN 978-0-545-66706-7 — ISBN 978-0-545-66707-4 1. Witnesses — Juvenile
fiction. 2. Witnesses — Protection — Juvenile fiction. 3. German shepherd dog —
Juvenile fiction. 4. Grandmothers — Juvenile fiction. 5. Friendship — Juvenile fiction.
6. Spokane County (Wash.) — Juvenile fiction. [1. Witnesses — Fiction. 2. Witnesses —
Protection — Fiction. 3. German shepherd dog — Fiction. 4. Dogs — Fiction.
5. Grandmothers — Fiction. 6. Friendship — Fiction. 7. Spokane County (Wash.) —
Fiction.] I. Title.
 PZ7.D727593Mi 2014
 813.6 — dc23
                                                                    2014005037

10 9 8 7 6 5 4 3 2 1   14 15 16 17 18

Printed in the U.S.A.   23
First edition, September 2014
Book design by Kristina Iulo

For Miss Jordan Kimmerly and her 2012 sixth-grade class at Marvista Elementary School. Your insightful questions, comments, and critiques made this a better book.

Chapter One

I DIDN'T know how to make the little girl stop crying.

She hovered against the wall of the North Shore Children's Center, her bunny print blanket wrapped around her, big tears splashing down her chubby cheeks. She'd been here three days and cried nearly all the time. I didn't know her story, or even her name, but it about drove me crazy that I couldn't figure out a way to make her feel better. I knew she was probably just scared, and who could blame her? Being here made me want to cry, too. But you can get away with stuff at four that you can't at twelve.

I bounced a curled knuckle against my bottom lip and wondered if there were any games on my phone she might like to play with. Or I could show her my snow globe. What little kid wouldn't think a snow globe was cool? It was at least worth a shot. But before I could duck back inside my room to grab it, the sharp *tap-tap-tap* of Miss Austin's high heels made me stop. She rounded the corner, her red dress stretched tight against her wide hips. She caught sight of me watching from the end of the hall and wiggled her fingers. "Oh, there you are, Poppy. I was just coming to find you."

Her words gave me a jolt, though I couldn't think of anything I'd done wrong.

She paused long enough to swoop the little girl into her arms as she passed, patting her back and mumbling in her ear. Her big hoop earrings jiggled and danced with each step until she stopped in front of me. "I wanted to let you know that your grandma was released from the hospital today and moved to the Huckleberry Home."

It's a funny thing how fast your brain can work, because the instant I heard the word *released*, my heart just about seized up with happiness. If Grandma Beth had been released, that meant she was out . . . free . . . it meant she was coming to get me. But then almost as fast, my brain told me that Miss Austin had continued to talk after the word *released*, that she'd said something about the Huckleberry Home, and my heart loosened again. "But . . . isn't that a nursing home?"

"It's one of Spokane's best."

"But she doesn't need a nursing home. She's getting better."

"She's made some progress, yes. That's why the doctor released her from the hospital. But she's going to continue suffering the effects of her stroke for quite a while."

"Then I'll take care of her, at *our* home."

Miss Austin sighed. She shifted the little girl in her arms. "Poppy, your grandma can't walk, bathe, or dress herself without assistance. Now I know you love her dearly, but until she can do those things for herself again, she needs more help than you can give."

I clenched my hands to keep from jerking those bouncy hoops from her ears. How did she know what I could or couldn't do? "Where is this place?"

"Downtown, near Freemont Field."

"Can you take me to see her?"

"Of course. Right after school tomorrow. How's that?"

Tomorrow? Tears burned my eyes. It had been ten days since Grandma Beth's stroke, and I'd only been allowed to visit her twice. And now they'd shipped her off to an old people's home. "I have to go now," I said. "She probably needs me."

"I'm sorry, hon. I have a meeting with Health and Welfare in twenty minutes. Tomorrow's the best I can do. And besides, your grandma probably needs time to settle in. Meet me here at three-thirty, okay?" She bent her head toward the little girl. "And now, what should we do with you, little miss Erin? How about if we go find you a cartoon to watch?" She turned and tapped off down the hall.

I ducked back inside my room, sure I'd burst open with the unfairness of it all. I didn't even have the phone number to the nursing home. How would I know if Grandma Beth was okay? Nobody else would be checking on her.

My roommate, Sidney, was sprawled on her bed — only about six feet from mine — flipping through a *Glamour Girl* magazine. Which was the funniest thing, because Sidney was the last girl on earth who I'd think of as glamorous. She glared at me with her beady little eyes as though she could read my mind. "Sounds like your grandma isn't doing so hot."

I looked away. I tried to make eye contact with Sidney as little as possible. "She's doing okay," I said.

"Don't sound like Miss A. thinks so."

"Well, she barely knows her." I turned toward my bed and stopped short. I stared at the wrinkled blue bedspread with a panicky feeling. My cell phone was gone. I'd left it lying on the pillow when I'd stepped out into the hall to check on Erin. I patted my pockets just in case and took a quick glance around the cramped room. Socks, Skittles wrappers, used tissues — all of it Sidney's garbage.

"Something wrong?" she asked.

I swallowed, and my heart started thumping like crazy, because I could tell from her tone of voice that she knew *exactly* what was wrong. I slowly faced her. "You don't know where my phone is, do you?"

She grunted. "No. I don't keep track of your stuff."

"But it was . . . right here, on the bed, a minute ago."

She flipped a page of her magazine, and a little smile lifted one corner of her mouth. "Well, you know, they're always telling us not to leave valuables lying around."

My knees started shaking. "You have it, don't you?"

Sidney lowered her magazine. "You wanna search me? Go for it."

I wanted to do a lot more than search her. I wanted to tie her in knots and shove her through the tiny little screened window above our beds. But the truth was, Sidney was twice my size and ten times meaner. Just accusing her took all the courage I had.

I nearly bit my tongue in half trying not to cry. My cell phone was the only connection I had with Grandma Beth — now she wouldn't even be able to call me. What if she didn't like the Huckleberry Home? What if they weren't taking care of her and she needed help? I couldn't leave her all alone like that. I had to check on her now — not tomorrow afternoon.

I dropped to my knees and groped under the mattress for my red mitten. I turned it upside down and let the coins clink into my palm — three dollars and twenty-six cents. It wasn't enough for a taxi, but it would buy bus fare.

Outside the center, the front gate stood open for the last of the kids straggling back from school. It was open from 7:00 to 7:30 each morning, and from 3:00 to 3:30 each afternoon. Any other time you needed a special pass. Nobody paid attention as I trotted past the paved entryway and crossed the grassy field to the sidewalk.

My timing must have been about perfect, because I'd barely reached the nearest bus stop when a Spokane city bus huffed and hissed its way to the curb. One whole side of the bus was painted with a grinning lady wearing a milk mustache, and it made me remember all the times Grandma Beth and I had walked to the Handy Mart for milk. It was our Saturday-afternoon ritual. First the dairy aisle, then the produce section, and finally the bakery to buy a snack for the way home — an apple fritter for me, and a maple bar for Grandma Beth.

I pushed the memory from my mind as I climbed onto the bus so that I wouldn't end up crying in front of a bunch of strangers. I tried to find Freemont Field on the city maps posted above the seats, but the print was small and people jostled around, blocking my view.

I knew that running off had probably been one of those bad decisions Grandma Beth always referred to as impulsive. *Think things through, Poppy. You'll have less to regret.* It's what she told me the time I let a girl in class borrow my jacket because she thought it was cute, and I had to bug her for a week until she finally got around to bringing it back. Or the time I brought home a litter of abandoned kittens even though I knew pets weren't allowed at our apartment.

It's not that I *tried* to be impulsive. It's just that sometimes a decision that seemed so right at the time, turned out to be not so right a little later. I closed my eyes and tried to remember exactly what Miss Austin had said about the Huckleberry Home. But the details were all jumbled up with my anger over Sidney and my cell phone, and I couldn't remember much of anything right then.

The man sitting beside me was focused on his tablet. "Excuse me, sir," I said. "Could you tell me where Freemont Field is?"

"I think it's at the end of the route," he said, "at Mission and Regal, maybe?"

Maybe? "Okay. Thank you."

The driver called out the choice of stops. I sat stiff in my seat and tried not to worry about what would happen if I got off at the wrong place. It seemed to take a long time, but I finally caught the word *Regal*, and I made my way forward, clutching the seats for balance.

There wasn't much chance for second-guessing, because as soon as I hopped off, the doors flapped shut and the bus roared away. I coughed my way through the diesel fumes and over to the sidewalk.

In front of me stood a park and baseball diamond, chain-linked all the way around, with a big sign in front — CHIEF GARRY PARK. Across the street stretched a giant metal building that said FREEMONT STEEL, plus a few older houses — nothing that looked like a nursing home. I stared at the metal building. Freemont Steel sounded a lot like Freemont Field. What had Miss Austin really said? Why didn't I get better directions? I should've at least grabbed my sweatshirt. I took a breath of the cool, pine-scented air and tried not to panic.

Four little black-capped chickadees peered down at me from an electric wire, and seeing them made me feel instantly better. It was my job to fill the bird feeder at home, and most of our visitors were chickadees. I smiled up at them. "Hey, guys. Ever hear of the Huckleberry Home?"

I fished in my pocket for some ChapStick and started off down the sidewalk. I wandered around for a long time, until I found a neighborhood of fancier homes with small lawns and pots of frosted petunias on the porches. I stopped two joggers and a lady on a scooter, but none of them had heard of the Huckleberry Home. Each time I smiled and said thanks, like it was no big deal, but inside I was getting quivery with worry.

Finally, I came to a corner gas station with a flashing neon sign advertising snacks and pop. My stomach growled like it could read. I pushed through the double glass doors and scanned the display of candy bars. I heard Grandma Beth's voice again. *If you have to eat candy, at least eat a little protein with your sugar.* I picked out a Snickers bar and walked up to the cashier. "Have you ever heard of the Huckleberry Home?"

"Sure have," she said with a warm smile.

My heart almost melted with relief. "Really?"

"Yep. My aunt Margo lives there. It's right next to Memorial Hospital."

"Memorial Hospital?" I echoed. "Well, is it very far from here?"

"Oh, I'd say about four miles."

The look on my face must've given me away. The cashier squinted and scooted up her glasses. "Are you okay, kiddo? You're not lost or anything, are you?"

Something about her kind face made me want to blurt everything out, to tell her how perfectly normal my life had been up until Grandma Beth's stroke. How we'd lived together and taken care of each other and done just fine. How the main things I'd worried about were passing math and convincing Luke Cleary that he wasn't the only sixth grader who liked country music — that I liked it, too.

But I didn't tell the cashier anything, because you could never be sure how an adult was going to react to things. I ducked my head. "I'm fine," I said and bumped the candy bar toward her. "This is all I need."

She took the little pile of coins I dropped in her hand, hesitated, and then handed the money back. "It's on me today."

"It is? Thanks," I said, giving her a shaky smile and hurrying outside before she could ask any more questions. I ripped the wrapper off the candy bar and took a big bite. Gooey sweetness filled my mouth and made me feel better, but not for long. If the Huckleberry Home was four miles away, it might as well be forty. I didn't have enough money for more bus fare. But I could feel the cashier watching me through the window and knew I couldn't just stand there looking lost. She might come out and ask me more questions. Or maybe she'd think I was a runaway and call the cops. The thought made me giggle. I guess I kind of *was* a runaway.

I threw my candy wrapper in the garbage and walked a few blocks past the gas station. After a while, I stumbled across a school playground and slumped on the bottom of the slide to rest my throbbing feet. Huge trees circled the playground. I loved big trees, especially Ponderosa pine and Douglas fir — loved their sharp, fresh smell and the way they endured wind and snow and lightning. Grandma Beth said old trees were a marvel, that if only they could talk, they'd amaze us with their wisdom. She always contributed to the Arbor Day Foundation, and I couldn't remember how many times she'd read me *The Giving Tree* when I was a little kid. It was still on my bookshelf at home.

I sure wished for some of that old-tree wisdom right then. My stomach still rumbled, and a light wind brought goose bumps to my arms. I closed my eyes and quit fighting the tears that had been threatening all afternoon. Why hadn't I just waited for Miss Austin to take me to the Huckleberry Home? Now I'd have to call her for a ride, and probably get a lecture. She'd probably make sure Grandma Beth heard about it, too.

I patted my pocket for my cell phone . . . and then remembered. Maybe the friendly cashier would let me use hers. I headed back to the mini-mart feeling defeated, and wondering how I'd ever get my phone back from Sidney.

I'd just started across the blacktop of the gas station parking lot when a loud *boom* made my whole body go rigid. A lady screamed. A man pumping gas threw an arm over his head. The way his mouth made a big O shape made me giggle — didn't he realize it was probably just a firecracker left over from the Fourth of July? Fireworks were illegal in Spokane County, because of the danger of forest fire, but people always set them off anyway.

But then a second *boom* sounded, loud enough to make my chest vibrate, and I was suddenly thinking gunshot and not fireworks.

I realized I was standing in the middle of the parking lot, which was probably not the safest place to be. I sprinted around the back side of the mini-mart and flattened myself against the brick wall. I didn't notice the back door just a few feet away until it flew open. A bony man with a long, drooping mustache burst out, a gun clutched in his hand.

12

He jerked around, panicked, and our eyes locked.

I broke out in a cold sweat.

My legs turned to rubber, and I dropped into a crouch. I put my hands in front me. "Don't," I whimpered. "Please . . . don't."

An awful heartbeat passed.

The man covered the ten feet between us in a flash. He bent over me, so close I could smell the stink of his breath. "Who are you?"

"P-Priscilla," I whispered. "Priscilla Parker."

He pressed a black-gloved hand against my mouth and glared at me. I'd never seen anyone with eyes like his — damp and overly bright. More like glowing lights instead of eyes. "A smart kid would keep her mouth shut," he said. "And an idiot would talk. Which are you?"

I tried to say *smart*, but I couldn't move my lips with the way his hand was pushed up against them. A car door slammed nearby, and he dropped his hand, whirled around, and scaled the wooden fence that separated the gas station from the rocky base of a hill.

I collapsed onto the black asphalt and tried to keep my stomach from coming out of my mouth. Noise came from the other side of the building — terrified voices and the slap of shoes on pavement. I jammed my hands into my armpits and focused on breathing. The haunting wail of sirens filled the air a few minutes later, but I was still too afraid to move.

"Hey, kid! Let's see your hands."

The gruff voice scared me so bad I banged my head against the bricks. A police officer eyed me from the corner, his gun pointed toward the ground. Another man stood beside him, taller, not in a uniform.

I raised my hands and started to cry. "I thought he was gonna shoot me," I blurted.

"Who?" both men asked.

"The g-g-guy with the g-g-gun," I stuttered, pointing to the fence. "He went that way."

"Get K-9 out here," the taller man ordered. He watched the officer scurry back around the front of the building, then he came over and squatted in front of me. He wore a badge clipped to his belt and a dark brown leather jacket that smelled like fresh dirt after a rainstorm. "I'm Detective Trey Brannigan," he said. "What's your name?"

"Priscilla — Poppy."

His eyebrows went up. "Poppy? Like the flower?"

I nodded.

"And your last name?"

"Parker."

He smiled. "Well, Poppy Parker, you can put your hands down now."

I tried to brush my tears away, but my hands were shaking so bad they bumped all around like they weren't part of me.

"You're okay," he said. "Everything's gonna be all right." He stood, offered a hand, and pulled me up. "Are you here with somebody?"

I shook my head. A wave of dizziness made me sway.

He put out an arm to steady me. "You're okay," he repeated. "Do you have a cell phone to call your parents?"

"No. And you can't call them anyway."

"Why's that?"

I wondered where to start. "It's kind of a long story."

"Hmm," he said. He scratched a sideburn. "Well, in that case, let's go find a place to talk."

Police officers swarmed around the other side of the gas station. Red and blue strobe lights flashed through the early dusk, and bright yellow caution tape twisted in the breeze. It looked just like the set of a TV cop show. An ambulance crew pulled a white sheet over someone on a stretcher.

"Oh, no," I breathed. "Is that the lady who works here?"

Detective Brannigan put a hand on my shoulder. "Come with me."

I stepped away from him as the panic surged through me. "He shot her, didn't he? Is she gonna be okay? She was really nice to me." I waited a few seconds for his answer before looking up at him. "Is she gonna be okay?"

He hesitated, like he was carefully weighing his words, then shook his head. "No. Afraid not."

I remembered the cashier's friendly smile, and my throat burned. I started to shake even worse. People hovered behind the caution tape, pointing, talking in hushed voices, and recording everything with their phones. There was motion everywhere, too much motion. Another wave of dizziness washed over me. "I don't feel so good."

"Yeah, scary stuff has that effect," Detective Brannigan said. He slipped his leather jacket off and the weight of it settled over my shoulders. I didn't realize how cold I was until I felt the warmth on my bare arms. "Come on," he said, "let's go sit for a few minutes."

He guided me over to a squad car and opened the back door. "Hop in," he said. Then he went around to the other side and climbed in beside me.

I slumped against the seat and studied the crisscrossing pattern of the metal barrier separating the front seat from the back. I realized where I was — sitting in an actual, real police car. I tried to swallow back a nervous giggle, but it slipped out anyway. "I've never been in a police car."

"Glad to hear that. So tell me what you were doing out behind the gas station."

His question sounded simple enough, but the answer was so complicated I didn't know where to start. I wondered if I was in trouble for running away? Was it against the law? "I was just trying to find my grandma."

"Hmm. Your grandma has a thing for gas stations?"

It took my tired brain a few seconds to realize he was trying to be funny. I looked up in surprise, and he smiled. He had thick brownish-gray hair that kicked up on his shirt collar, and eyes the color of strong coffee. The kind Grandma Beth liked to drink — one sugar, no cream. I started to tell him about her stroke, and how she'd been moved to the Huckleberry Home, and about getting off at the wrong stop, and finally about what had happened at the gas station.

He listened to the whole thing without interrupting. "Well," he said. "I guess I could see why you felt the need to find your grandma. She sounds like quite a woman."

"She is," I said, and the emotion rolled into my voice.

"We've been together since I was a baby. And it's not right that they stuck me in the kids' shelter when I should be taking care of her."

He didn't respond. I rested my head against the seat. "Can you call my social worker to come get me? Her name's Miss Austin."

"Suppose you tell me how good a look you got at the suspect first."

I thought of the man's weird eyes and the awful smell of his breath and felt another wave of nausea. "A good one."

"If I showed you a picture, do you think you'd recognize him?"

I nodded. "I'm good with details. I like to draw."

"Really? You draw people?"

"No. Dogs mostly."

"Dogs, huh? Okay. The suspect didn't speak to you, did he?"

"He asked who I was."

Detective Brannigan rubbed a thumb and forefinger over his bottom lip. "Yeah? What did you tell him?"

I searched his face. Even though his voice hadn't changed, I got the distinct feeling that I'd done something terribly wrong. "My name," I admitted softly.

"First and last?"

I nodded.

"All right. You stay put for a bit, and I'm gonna talk to a few people." He climbed out and then bent to smile at me. "Don't leave town, okay?"

A cold draft blew through the open doors of the squad car. I slipped my arms through the sleeves of his jacket as Detective Brannigan disappeared into the gas station. The ambulance was gone. I thought about the cheerful cashier and wanted to cry again. How could she be dead? I'd talked with her only an hour or two ago.

A mournful baying made me bolt up to see a black-and-tan bloodhound jump out of the backseat of another police car parked nearby. He wore a harness and a vest that said DOZER — SPOKANE COUNTY K-9 UNIT, and he wiggled around so excited I thought he might jump right out of his wrinkled skin. He shook his massive head and a line of drool went flinging across his handler's legs as the two of them disappeared around the building. Dozer was such a cool name for a dog. I wished I had my phone so I could take his picture and draw him later.

Miss Austin showed up soon after. I scrunched down in the seat and watched her scurry around in her bright red dress and high-heeled pumps. I felt a twinge of guilt for all the trouble I'd caused her. But still, if she'd only taken me to see Grandma Beth, I wouldn't be in this mess. She flitted around to different police officers until one of them finally pointed her toward Detective Brannigan. Then the two of them stood talking for a long time. The flashing lights made my head pound. I closed my eyes.

I opened them again when the familiar *tap-tap-tap* came close to the car. Miss Austin had a look of panic on her face. "Poppy! You had me so worried! Where in the world did you think you were going?"

"Just to see Grandma Beth."

"But I told you I'd take you tomorrow."

I sighed. "I know. I'm sorry. I was just worried she might need me. Can we go back to the center now? I'm really tired and hungry."

Detective Brannigan had come up behind her, and she glanced over her shoulder at him before answering. "I don't think you'll be going back right yet."

"What do you mean?"

Miss Austin moved aside, and Detective Brannigan knelt beside the door. "We need to go to the police station and get your story down, Poppy."

"But I already told you my story. Why do I need to go to the police station?"

He cleared his throat. "Because right now it seems you're the only person who can identify the suspect. That makes you pretty valuable."

I gaped at him. "That's crazy. There's a zillion people around here."

"Yeah, but they're all saying pretty much the same thing. The suspect had a mask on when he went in, but the cashier somehow pulled it off him before she was shot. Then he panicked and ran out the back door. So you really might have been the only one who saw his face."

It took me a minute to digest his words, but then I understood, and it felt like ants were running up and down my neck. "You think he might come after me?"

Detective Brannigan shook his head. "No, I don't think that. But we do want you someplace where we can keep an eye on you for a while."

Someplace? "But I have to see Grandma Beth." I looked at Miss Austin. "You'll still take me to see her, won't you? You promised."

"I'll make sure you see your grandma," Detective Brannigan said.

"When?"

"Tomorrow."

I wasn't sure if I could believe him or not, and it made me feel so helpless. "Do you really mean that?"

He met my gaze. "I don't say things I don't mean."

My chin trembled, and I slumped back against the seat. It felt like I'd been up for two days. "What time is it?"

"Six-fifty," he said.

Miss Austin fingered her hair. "I have a quick errand to run, Detective Brannigan. Can I just meet up with Poppy at the police station?"

"That'll be fine," he said.

"All right." She smiled at me. "I'll see you shortly, Poppy."

I didn't answer as she clicked away. What was there to say?

Chapter Two

TWO new officers came to the car. Detective Brannigan introduced them as Officer Ray Baxter and Officer Maria Córdoba. Officer Baxter wedged himself behind the steering wheel. He had a patch of gray fluffy hair and looked like he might be about ready to retire. Officer Córdoba had huge dark eyes and looked like she'd just graduated from high school. She shook my hand and told me to call her Maria before she slipped into the passenger seat. Detective Brannigan sat in back with me, and the four of us finally escaped the glaring lights of the gas station.

I closed my eyes and rubbed my neck. My muscles had been knotted for so many hours they'd forgotten how to relax, and my head throbbed like something fierce. But a few minutes later I felt my body swing left, and I looked to see that Officer Baxter had turned into the drive-thru lane of a McDonald's.

Detective Brannigan raised his eyebrows at me. "You said you were hungry. You like Happy Meals, or are you too grown-up for that?"

Officer Baxter hooted. "A hot fudge sundae for me, as long as you promise not to tell Flora. She'd skin me alive."

Maria laughed. "Oh, jeez, Ray, as if she doesn't already know how you eat."

"So what's your answer?" Detective Brannigan asked me.

I fumbled for the change in my pocket. "I love Happy Meals. But I don't think I have enough money."

"Don't worry about the money. Do you want a hamburger or cheeseburger?"

"Cheeseburger, please."

"Two Quarter Pounders," he called into the intercom after the others had ordered, "a cheeseburger Happy Meal, and a large coffee." He pulled a ten from his wallet.

My neck muscles relaxed a little. "Thanks, Detective Brannigan."

"You're welcome. And you can call me Trey, okay?"

The rhyme made me smile. "Okay."

As soon as I unwrapped my cheeseburger, I realized I wasn't just hungry — I was starving. But I chewed slowly, savoring each greasy bite. I was so focused on the food that it took me a while to notice Trey studying me. I'd caught him doing it before, when we were at the gas station. At the time I figured he'd been thinking other thoughts, just looking my way without realizing. But now I knew he wasn't, and it gave me a start. "What?" I asked.

"Nothing," he said, and turned away to take a bite of his hamburger.

When we reached the police station, Trey led the way through an electronic door marked POLICE ENTRANCE ONLY. The lobby was bright with fluorescent lights and cluttered with desks and file cabinets. Half a dozen police officers worked on computers or talked above the noisy drone of a dispatcher's voice coming from a scanner.

Trey led us down a short, tiled hallway, past a door that said PROPERTY ROOM and another that said ROLL CALL AND BRIEFING. I'd only been in a police station once in my whole life — for a field trip in second grade. An officer had taken us on a tour of the building. He'd showed us how handcuffs worked and let us crowd into a real, live holding cell and gave us suckers when the tour ended. It'd been so cool and exciting. This time it wasn't either. My neck started to tighten again.

We climbed a flight of stairs, and Trey turned into an office with brown patterned carpet, an old mahogany desk, and a fish tank. I wandered over to look at the tropical fish. They were all vivid blues and oranges and yellows, and their gills billowed gently as they swam in and out of a jungle of fake seaweed.

"What kind of fish is this fat orange one?" I asked Maria. But before she could answer, a man strode into the room. He was squat and bald except for a chin full of white whiskers. He came right over and offered me his hand. "Captain Pete Ross," he announced in a booming voice that made my headache worse. He glanced around the room. "Parents?"

"Poppy's legal guardian is her grandmother," Trey said. "But she's been staying at the North Shore Children's Center for the past week and a half. Her caseworker is on the way."

Captain Ross waved me toward a velvet-padded chair. Then he grabbed another for himself and sat down facing me, knee to knee. He winked at me. "Poppy, huh? Cute name. How're you feeling about now, kiddo? A little nervous maybe? Uptight?"

"I'm okay."

"Good. We're all a friendly bunch here. Maria's the only one you need to watch out for."

She wiggled her eyebrows. "Thanks, sir."

"No problem," he said. "So, tell me, Poppy, how come you ended up at the kids' center?"

"I'm not sure," I mumbled.

Captain Ross raised his eyebrows, and I could tell he expected more explanation.

"My grandma had a stroke," I said. "She had to go to the hospital, and they wouldn't let me stay home alone."

"How long have you lived with your grandmother?"

"Since I was almost one."

"And your folks?"

I jabbed my thumbnails into the chair's soft velvet cushion. "They died a long time ago," I said. "In Africa."

The captain's smile faded a bit, but he didn't give me the dropped-jaw, shocked look that most people did. "Africa?"

"Yeah. In Botswana."

"Hmm. What kind of things do you like to do?" he asked.

I relaxed my thumbs. "Anything with animals. And I like to draw, especially dogs."

"Yeah? I had a dog once, but the wife made me get rid of him."

The way he said it made my heart catch a little. "I used to have a dog, too," I said. "A chocolate Lab named Lucy. But we had to find her a new home when Grandma Beth and I moved into our apartment."

I rubbed my eyes. It felt like tiny fists were punching them from behind. But then Miss Austin showed up a few minutes later, and things got even worse. Captain Ross made me rehash every single second of my afternoon, from the time I went into the gas station to buy the Snickers bar until Trey found me out behind the building. Sometimes he asked for the same information with two different questions, and even though he was recording me, he kept making me back up so he could jot things on a notepad.

I couldn't see Miss Austin or Maria, but I knew they were in the room from the occasional shuffling of feet or creak of a chair. Trey sat on the corner of the big desk, his arms crossed over his chest. He didn't say a word during the whole interview, but he studied me a lot.

When the clock above the fish tank read 9:15, Miss Austin cleared her throat. "Captain Ross, I really need to be getting home, and I'm sure Poppy's exhausted. Is there a way we can continue this tomorrow?"

"Absolutely," he said. "We're done anyway."

Trey glanced at me. "Captain, can I speak with you and Miss Austin in the other room for a minute?"

Captain Ross seemed to hesitate for a few seconds before nodding. "Sure. Of course." He patted my knee as he stood. "You're a trouper, know that? A real trouper. You did great."

He led the way out of the room with Miss Austin and Trey following. Maria came up and massaged my shoulders. "You're tight as a drum. I bet you're more than sick of this."

"Sick to death."

"Want some hot cocoa?"

What I wanted most was for her to keep massaging my shoulders, but I nodded anyway. "Sure."

"Okay. Be right back."

I stood and dug in my pocket for my ChapStick. A plastic grocery bag sat on the floor near Miss Austin's chair, a pink-and-gray blanket peeking out the top. I walked over for a closer look. It was my flannel blanket — the one Grandma Beth had sewn for me when I was seven. Underneath were some clean clothes and my toothbrush, snow globe, and art pad. I stared at the bag with an unsettled feeling. Why would Miss Austin bring my stuff here? Did she know something I didn't? I thought about the long talk she'd had with Trey at the gas station, and that's when I noticed the muffled voices of Trey and Captain Ross drifting down the hall. I couldn't pick out the words, but neither of them sounded happy. A tingle of alarm zipped down my spine.

Captain Ross said I'd done good, that I'd been a real trouper, so what was there to argue about? I peeked out into the empty corridor and then crept a few steps toward the voices.

". . . do it in a heartbeat if the budget allowed," Captain Ross said. "But it doesn't."

Trey's voice was lower, harder to hear, but I caught something about three dozen kids being too many, and all he needed was one officer.

"Move on, Brannigan," Captain Ross said, clear as a bell. And then I heard soft footsteps, and I darted back into the interview room.

Maria rounded the corner with two steaming Styrofoam cups. Her smile faded when she saw me. "Are you okay, Poppy?"

I poked a finger toward the door. "They're fighting about me. Trey and the Captain. I can hear them."

Her face relaxed. "Oh, no worries. They butt heads over all kinds of things."

I wasn't sure that made me feel better. "They do?"

"Sure. Captain Ross gets the final say, of course. But he's always bantering with somebody, especially Detective Brannigan. They're probably trying to decide what to do with you."

She said it so casual, like it was no big deal at all. But it made me feel like I was stumbling around in the dark, not sure the floor would be there when I took my next step. All I'd wanted was to see Grandma Beth. How did I ever end up at the police station, with two strangers trying to decide what to do with me? "What does that mean, exactly?"

Maria gave a dismissive shrug. "Oh, you know, there's always a bunch of red tape with these kinds of things."

I *didn't* know, but I was too tired to ask.

Maria held out a cup of cocoa, but I was still wearing Trey's jacket, and I had to pull the sleeve back to find my hand. She smiled. "He must really like you. I don't see him without that jacket very often."

The tips of my ears got hot, but it was a good kind of warmth — the kind that made me feel better. So did the cocoa. It was creamy and sweet and triggered a bright memory. Grandma Beth and me sitting in the backyard, studying our star maps while we sipped our own hot chocolate. *See there*, I heard her say, *that's Orion. The one that looks like Grandma's big chili pot.*

After what seemed like forever, Captain Ross and Trey came back into the room, trailed by Miss Austin. I tensed up again. "Guess what?" Captain Ross grinned like he had the best news in the world. "You get to spend the night right here in the cop shop with us."

I groaned. This had been the most mixed-up day of my life, my neck and shoulders felt like they were fused together, and my head was killing me. "Why can't I just go back to the center?"

Miss Austin clutched her purse with both hands. "It'll just be best if you stay here, Poppy. But it's only for tonight. We'll have something better worked out for you by tomorrow."

"Something better *where*?"

She gave Captain Ross a helpless look.

"We're still working out the details on that one," he said.

I couldn't believe it. Neither of them were making any sense. My eyelids burned with tears. "All I wanna do is see my grandma."

Maria put an arm around my shoulders. "It's gonna be okay, Poppy. I know you're feeling overwhelmed right now. But I promise it's not so bad here." She looked at Captain Ross. "Can I stay with her, sir? I can do my paperwork in here instead of in the report room."

"Sure," he said, looking relieved by her offer. "I'll get a replacement for Ray."

Miss Austin smiled brightly. "See, no reason to worry at all. Everything will be fine. Try and get some rest, and I'll see you tomorrow. Okay?" She turned and made her way from the room before I had a chance to say anything.

"I'll need a few things from Supply," Maria said.

"Of course," Captain Ross said. "Let's go get what you need right now."

Maria gave me a squeeze. "Just relax a minute, and I'll be right back." She followed the captain out into the hall.

I dropped back into the velvet-padded chair, set my empty cup on the carpet, and closed my eyes. I heard Trey come over and kneel in front of me. "Hey, Poppy. Look at me a minute."

I wanted to tell him that I was too tired to look at him, to just please go away and leave me alone. But there was something about his voice that made him hard to ignore. I sniffled and opened my eyes.

"You know what you told us about losing your parents?"

I hated when people used the word *losing* like that. It made me think of a little puppy that accidentally wanders off and gets lost. "I didn't really lose them," I said. "They left me."

A flicker of surprise crossed his dark eyes, and I figured he probably thought I was an awful person. He tipped his head. "Well," he said, "you told me that cashier from the convenience store was nice to you. So I thought you'd want to know her name was Lindsay, and she had a three-year-old daughter."

This caught my attention. An image of the little girl at the center filled my mind, and my fingers clenched into fists. "Oh, no. She has a dad, too, I hope."

"She does. But her mom's still gone. So for her sake, and for everyone else's, we need to get this guy off the street. And you can help us. You understand?"

"Dozer couldn't track him?"

"He lost the trail at the river."

"So, the guy's out there . . . free?"

"Yeah, but you can bet he's scared. And scared people do stupid things. Right now we've got this little window of opportunity when our chance of nabbing him is good. So tomorrow we'd like to show you some pictures and see if anyone looks familiar. And if not, we'd like you to help our police artist come up with a sketch so we can plaster his face all over Spokane. Can you do that?"

I looked down at the rug and thought of the cashier's little girl. Three was so young. Practically a baby. Would she understand what had happened — that her mom had been *taken* from her? Or would she simply think her mom had left by choice . . . like my mom?

I took a shaky breath. "Okay. I'll look at the pictures. But can you *please* take me to see my grandma first?"

"Fair enough," he said.

Maria and Captain Ross brought in a rollaway cot and some blankets. Trey stood and ruffled my hair. "Sorry about all this, Tiger. Try and get some rest, huh?"

Tiger? No one had ever called me that. I liked it. I reluctantly slipped off his jacket and handed it to him.

Captain Ross gave me a thumbs-up. "You're the best, Poppy. One in a million. Really appreciate your cooperation."

Maria set up the cot on the far side of the room and turned off the overhead fluorescent light. "Sorry about the desk lamp. But I need enough light to do paperwork."

"It's fine," I said. "I just wanna lie down. Can you stay all night?"

"Yep. This is my normal shift anyway. But usually I'm out on patrol with Ray."

The bag from Miss Austin still sat by the door. I went over and pulled out my flannel blanket. I pressed it to my nose, longing for the sweet smell of the lavender drops Grandma Beth always added to the washing machine. But it didn't smell like lavender anymore, it didn't smell like home at all. It smelled like the center, and it made me want to cry again.

Was Grandma Beth okay? Did her left hip ache like it often did at home? Had she tried to call me? Would she feel like I'd abandoned her? I wrapped the blanket around me and lay down on the cot with my back to Maria.

I wanted to sleep in the worst way, but as soon as I closed my eyes, I started remembering the gunshots, and the feel of the man's gloved hand against my mouth, and the lady lying on the white gurney. So I forced myself to think about Grandma Beth some more. I wondered if she was missing me and our bedtime routine — the one where she'd open her huge book of famous quotations and pick out our "nightly three" to share. Some were funny, some made you think, and some were just plain dumb. But it didn't matter — I loved hearing them anyway.

Grandma Beth had been gone eleven nights. We were thirty-three quotations behind.

Chapter Three

I WAS afraid I wouldn't get to see Grandma Beth until after school the next day, but when I woke in the morning, Trey told me I didn't have to go to school. He drove me to the Huckleberry Home in his own car. It was a black Pontiac GT with chrome wheels and a cool little camera that showed what was behind you when you backed up. I told him how much Grandma Beth would love one of those cameras. How she'd been terrified of backing up ever since she was learning to drive at fifteen and had taken out a whole section of the neighbor's newly painted fence.

He smirked. "A fence? Shoot, I backed into my buddy's Mustang the night we graduated high school."

"Really! What'd he say?"

Trey shook his head. "Don't think I better repeat it."

I giggled as I drummed my fingers on the armrest,

impatient to get to Grandma Beth. I tried to decide what to tell her about what had happened at the gas station. The last thing I wanted to do was scare her and slow down her recovery time.

"I don't think I'm gonna say anything about yesterday," I announced, shortly before we got to the nursing home.

Trey raised his eyebrows. "You have to."

His abrupt answer caught me off guard. "Why?"

"Because she's your legal guardian. She needs to know what's going on."

"But it'll just scare her. She always worries too much about me anyway."

"I understand that, Poppy. But you have to tell her, regardless."

My stomach fluttered. He was wrong, but I didn't know how to tell him that. It's not like I had a lot of experience arguing with adults, especially one I barely knew . . . especially a cop. "How come?" I finally asked, sounding as unsure as I felt. "What difference does it make?"

"It's not about whether it makes a difference. It's about you being a minor, and her right to know what's going on with her granddaughter."

"But she'll *see* I'm okay. And she knows I've been staying at the center."

"Don't you think she'll wonder what I'm doing there?"

I swallowed. I hadn't thought about that. "Well, can I at least not tell her about . . ." I started to say *Lindsay*, but somehow it seemed too personal. ". . . about the cashier?"

Trey sighed. "I understand why you don't want to, Poppy. But she needs to know, and it'll trouble her less if she hears it from you."

"And if I *don't* tell her?"

"Then I'll have to."

Frustration flowed through me and made my knee start bouncing on its own. "Why should *you* get to decide? You don't even know her."

But as soon as the words were out, my face got hot enough to melt. I wanted to dive under the floor mats. I couldn't believe I'd said that to an adult. Grandma Beth would be furious with me. Then I did something just as bad — I started to laugh.

Trey gave me a somber look that filled my whole body with pins and needles. I slapped a hand to my mouth. "Sorry. Sometimes I laugh at stuff that's not funny."

Grandma Beth said my nervous-laughter thing was genetic — that I'd inherited the tendency from my mom. She told me that when my dad asked my mom to marry him, she'd burst out laughing, and it had really upset him.

I couldn't tell if Trey was upset or not, because he didn't say anything. He just turned his focus back to the road and gave the steering wheel a few solid taps with his thumb.

The Huckleberry Home looked like a restaurant from the outside. It was a long, boxy building, white with purple trim, with a steaming huckleberry pie painted near the front entrance. But as soon as we stepped inside, I knew it wasn't a restaurant — it smelled just like the hospital.

A lady at the front desk asked us to sign the guest book. She handed me a lacy white feather pen like you'd see at a wedding, then pointed us toward room 24. I half walked, half skipped down the beige hallway. But as soon as I rounded the doorway to Grandma's room, I stopped. She was dozing, her head tipped back on the pillow, her mouth open and droopy on the right side. I was embarrassed for Trey to see her like that, so I hurried over and gave her hand a squeeze. She opened her green eyes with a start and focused on me. "Oh, Poppy, honey."

I leaned close to kiss her cheek and caught a whiff of the peppermint denture cream she used to brush her false teeth. It smelled just like our bathroom at home. "I'm here, Grandma Beth. How are you? Is this place better than the hospital?"

"I've been better, sweetie. But I'm sure glad to see you. I tried to call you three times yesterday."

"You did?" Suddenly I was even madder at Sidney. "I'm really sorry. I didn't have my phone."

"Oh, no. You didn't lose it, I hope."

"No. It got stolen."

"Stolen! Did you tell anyone?"

"I haven't had a chance yet. But I will."

"Who brought you?" she asked. "Miss Austin?"

I glanced over my shoulder. Trey leaned against the door-frame. "Uh, not exactly."

Grandma Beth pushed a button on her bed, and it raised her to a sitting position. "Oh, well, hello there," she said to Trey.

He stepped over and offered a hand. "Detective Trey Brannigan, ma'am. Nice to meet you."

Grandma held out her thin, fragile hand, and it disappeared inside of Trey's as they shook. "Detective?" she asked, sounding worried.

"Actually," I said quickly, "something kinda scary happened yesterday, Grandma. You probably won't believe it, but I saw a guy rob a gas station, and . . ." I hesitated, trying to pick words that would scare her the least. ". . . and a cashier got shot."

She pulled her hand from Trey's and fumbled for mine. "What! Oh my Lord, Poppy."

"No, don't worry. Everything's fine. But the police want me to look at some pictures to see if I can identify the guy who did it. That's why I'm not in school today."

Grandma Beth searched my face, seeming to digest that for a minute. "But why were you at the gas station? Were you with Miss Austin?"

I swallowed. "Uh, no, actually I was trying to find you."

Grandma Beth's eyes flashed. "Priscilla Parker! That's just the kind of impulsive decision I'm always warning you about."

I bit the inside of my bottom lip as heat rushed to my face. I'd expected a lecture, but it was way worse with Trey standing there. "I was just worried about you is all."

Her face softened, and she gave my hand a gentle squeeze. "I know, honey. I'm sorry. I just want you to be safe."

Trey cleared his throat. "Speaking of keeping Poppy safe, Mrs. Parker, I was hoping to get your permission to take her to my mother's house for a few days."

I don't know if my mouth fell open, but it sure felt like it did. "What?"

"Your mother's?" Grandma Beth asked.

Trey nodded. "Poppy told the suspect her name. I want to keep tabs on her until we can find him, but the budget won't allow me to put a full-time officer at her school. And it would be pretty tough to keep track of her around all those kids anyway."

A shiver passed through me, and I saw the fear in Grandma Beth's eyes. "Ohhhh," she said. "I see."

"But what does your mom have to do with anything?" I asked.

"For one thing, she and I live in opposite ends of the same duplex, so I'll be right there. Plus," he added, with a smile, "Mom loves two things in this world: kids and dogs. She'll take in strays of any kind. She and Dad used to take in foster kids."

I tried to make sense of his words. "You think I'm a stray?"

He winked. "Figuratively speaking, of course."

Grandma Beth and I looked at each other. "How long would this be for?" she asked.

"Wish I had an answer to that," Trey said. "But I'm afraid I don't. Hopefully just temporarily. Until we find the guy."

"What about her schooling?"

"I'm sure Miss Austin could arrange to get her homework for her. She could do it at Mom's."

"And where exactly do you live?" she said.

"West Twenty-Fifth and South Howard."

I sucked in a breath. "Really? That's only like four blocks from our apartment." If I stayed there, I could go home and get my bike and come to see Grandma Beth whenever I wanted. I started to feel hopeful.

Grandma Beth nodded. "Well, Detective Brannigan, if that's what you think best, then of course you have my permission."

"Great. Thank you," Trey said. "I'll have Miss Austin bring you the necessary paperwork to sign." He took a step back and jerked his thumb toward the door. "Now I'll wait over here and let you two visit."

"Detective Brannigan?" Grandma Beth said. "You make sure you look after my Poppy for me. Please."

"Yes, ma'am. I'll do that."

I waited for Trey to move away, then lowered my face to Grandma Beth's. "So tell me what to do to get you out of here," I whispered.

Her eyes showed her disappointment. "I'm afraid I'm gonna have to stay for some time, honey. My right side is refusing to cooperate with me."

"It's okay," I said. "I can take care of you. I'll drop out of school for a little while and do whatever you need."

"You will do no such thing. Do you think I raised an honor student just to let her drop out in sixth grade?"

"I'm barely getting a C in math, Grandma. And I didn't mean drop out for good, just until you get better."

She snorted. "Not even for a day, Priscilla Marie. You'll stay in school and get good grades and make me proud. Is that understood?"

I gritted my teeth to keep the tears back, but they came anyway. "I'm not leaving you, Grandma. What can they do for you here that I can't do at home?"

She reached up with her left hand and smoothed the bangs from my eyes. "Well, for one thing, I can't walk without falling because my balance is all catawampus. Now, do you see Detective Brannigan over there?"

"Yeah."

"No. Take a look at him."

I glanced over at Trey. He was fooling around with his cell phone. "Okay," I said.

"Well, whenever I need to go someplace, they send in a big, strapping aide about his size to lift me in and out of a wheelchair. Now, do you think you could do that?"

I swallowed. "I'd figure out a way."

She chuckled. "And do you know what would happen if you tried? The same thing that happened when you and I carried that eighty-pound sack of chicken feed for Mr. Hankins. You remember that? We got it halfway to the shed and dropped it, and the whole thing burst open. We had cracked corn to kazoo."

I smiled in spite of myself. "Yeah, I remember. But I'd find a way."

She patted my cheek. "That's my Poppy, always trying to fix things. How about if we both just take one day at a time, and do the best we can. God be willing, maybe we'll be back together soon."

Maybe? The word sent a tingling chill through my whole body. "But what about stuff at home?"

"I asked Mrs. Gilly to keep an eye on the plants and to check the mail. Everything else will be fine for a while."

A smiling man entered the room, dressed in a dark blue shirt and pants, with a name card dangling from his neck. "Pardon me for interrupting, Bethany. I didn't know you had company."

Grandma Beth introduced him as Chad, and he pumped my hand. "You two visit as long as you like," he said. "But in about fifteen minutes the Mission Gospel Choir will be performing in the recreation room. They're pretty good, from what I hear."

"That sounds very nice," Grandma Beth said. "Would you like to stay, Poppy?"

I couldn't see Trey; he'd slipped out of the room. "I don't think I can, Grandma. You go listen for me." The idea of leaving her again made me feel sick inside. But I couldn't think of anything more to say with Chad in the room. I kissed her on the cheek again. "I'll get back just as soon as I can. Promise."

"You do that," she said.

Trey stood in the hall, studying the Western artwork on the walls. He seemed to sense me behind him and turned. "Ready?"

I knew I should answer him, but there was a whole mess of tears at the base of my throat, just waiting for the chance to come flooding out. I guess he could tell, because he turned and led the way down the hall and out to the car.

"So, tell me more about this missing cell phone," Trey said as we pulled back onto the street.

I rubbed my face. "It's not missing. I *know* who took it. The girl they make me room with."

"How do you know?"

"Because it was lying on my pillow when I stepped out into the hall. And a minute later it was gone. And she was the only other person there. Plus she's just an idiot anyway. Everybody's scared of her."

"Oh, yeah? What's her name?"

"Sidney something." I glanced over at him with a glimmer of hope. "Do you think you could get it back for me?"

"Maybe."

Maybe. There was that awful word again, the same one Grandma Beth had used. *Maybe* we'll be together again. Like she didn't really believe it. What if she didn't get better? What would happen to me? My heart started thumping like I'd been running.

Life with Grandma Beth had always been safe and predictable and . . . close somehow. Kind of like being zipped up in a warm sleeping bag, with the sides only inches away and no worries about falling out. But now, I felt like I'd been yanked from the sleeping bag and dropped into the middle of a great openness, miles away from any sides or walls. I was just floundering around with no control over anything anymore, and I hated that feeling. I'd been sure that if I could only visit Grandma Beth and make sure she was okay, I'd feel so much better. But I didn't feel better. All I felt was scared.

I glanced over at Trey. "Have you already told your mom about me?"

He nodded. "She's expecting you this afternoon."

"And you're sure she doesn't mind?"

"Trust me."

I sighed. At least it wasn't very far away. I started thinking again how easy it would be to go home and get my bike when I felt Trey looking at me. I glanced over and caught him. "Why do you stare at me like that?"

"Sorry. You just remind me of someone."

"Who?"

"It doesn't matter. It was a long time ago."

"If it doesn't matter, why don't you just answer the question?" He raised his eyebrows, and I gave him a sheepish grin. "You ask *me* lots of questions."

"Guess I can't argue with that," he said. "You look a lot like a little girl I used to know."

"I'm not little. I'm twelve."

"Okay. You look a lot like a *young* girl I used to know. You have the same eyes, the whole middle part of your face actually."

"Really? What's her name?"

His mouth pressed into a hard line, and I didn't think he was going to answer. "Virginia Sykes," he said.

Virginia. I briefly wondered why anybody would give their kid such an old-sounding name. "Does she live around here?"

"No."

That *no* was like a door slamming, and I knew better than to knock. "Okay," I said.

When Trey and I got back to the police station, he took me into Captain Ross's office and then sat with me as I scrolled through hundreds of pictures of suspects. But none of them looked like the guy at the gas station.

Another headache was coming on strong, and I rubbed my temples. "Sorry. I've looked at so many faces now I'm not sure if I'd recognize him."

"No problem," Trey said. "We'll take a break, and then I'll introduce you to our sketch artist. She's really good. You'll like her."

A few minutes later we were back in the interview room, where the fish bubbled in their tank. A woman rose from one of the velvet-padded chairs and came toward me, hand outstretched. She reminded me of a model.

"Hey, I'm Cindy Bradshaw. You must be Poppy?"

"You're the police artist?"

"Sure am. And I hear you're a bit of an artist yourself. Come on, let's just sit and visit."

The clock showed ten minutes after one. By two o'clock I began to think maybe Cindy had forgotten why she was there.

She propped a sketchpad on her lap and doodled something now and then, but she rarely asked anything about how the man at the gas station had looked. Instead, we talked about art, and dogs, and I told her how I'd always dreamed of illustrating kids' picture books. Once in a while Cindy threw in a quick question like, "Should I make the chin kind of pointed or more rounded?" or "Should I make the eyes close together or about average?" Then we'd go right back to talking about boy bands or who had the best pizza in Spokane.

Then abruptly, Cindy waved her pencil in the air with a flourish and said, "Okay, that about does it. Tell me what you think." She turned the sketchbook around.

It was like somebody shouted right in my face.

I was back at the gas station, cringing against the brick wall, staring through my fingers, feeling like I might pee myself.

"Pretty close?" Cindy asked gently.

"Real close," I breathed. "How did you do that?"

"*You* did it. You remembered all the right details. I'll go get this to Captain Ross so he can get the ball rolling." She flashed me a bright smile as she stood. "It's been awesome working with you, Poppy. I admire your courage. You're a lot of fun, too."

I sat there alone, my skin crawling. When the door swung open a minute later I must've jumped six inches straight up.

Trey frowned and raised his hands in surrender. "Take it easy there, Tiger, it's only me. What's going on?"

"Nothing," I said. "Guess I'm just a little jumpy is all."

"I see that. Cindy says you were great to work with. Thanks for your help."

"She's a really, really good artist."

"One of the best. We're lucky to have her. So, you about ready to get out of here and go meet my mom?"

"I guess. If you're really sure she's okay with it."

"Didn't I tell you to trust me?"

I fought back the urge to giggle. I *did* trust him, but I still felt like I was about to barge in on a party I hadn't been invited to.

Chapter Four

TREY coasted up alongside a single-story duplex. It was light blue with white shutters and matching window boxes stuffed with flowers. It looked like a nice place, but I really perked up when I saw the brown-and-white basset hound lying by the front door. "Is that your mom's dog?"

"One of 'em. That's Harvey."

I grabbed my bag and followed Trey through the chain-link gate into the yard. Harvey jogged over, giant ears bouncing and body swaying. I let him sniff my hand, and then knelt and squeezed his thick neck. "Hey, boy. Aren't you cute. What a good dog."

A heavy pink tongue shot out and slathered right across my mouth. "Whoa." I laughed. "Gross."

"Oh, Harvey," a lady's voice said, "where are your manners?"

A smiling woman came down the steps, dressed in black yoga pants and an Adidas workout shirt. Glasses dangled against her chest, held in place by a jeweled chain that looped around her neck.

"Mom," Trey said, "meet Poppy Parker."

She took one of my hands in both of hers. "I am so happy to meet you. I'm Marti Brannigan."

"Hi," I said as Harvey continued to sniff up and down my legs.

"I'm sorry. I hope you don't mind him."

"He's adorable." I said. "I love dogs."

A girl about my age rounded the corner of the house, pushing a wheelbarrow full of dirt and dried-up plants. Her hair was jet-black except for some brilliant pink highlights, and bare patches of skin peeked out from behind the rips in her skinny jeans. She came to an abrupt stop when she saw us.

"What is she doing here?" Trey asked under his breath.

"It's fine," Marti murmured. She smiled at the girl. "How are things coming, Lizzie?"

"I dug up the dahlias," she said. "Where do you want them?"

"There's a wooden crate just inside the garden shed. Go ahead and put them there for now, please." She draped an arm around my shoulders and nudged me forward. "Oh, and Lizzie, I'd like you to meet Poppy Parker."

Our eyes met. "Hey," I said.

The girl gave a barely perceptible nod before she backed up the wheelbarrow and disappeared again.

"What is she doing here?" Trey repeated. "She's supposed to be putting in her time at the shelter."

Marti clicked her tongue. "I know, TJ. But I needed some help getting the garden cleaned up for fall, and I didn't see any reason why she couldn't spend the afternoon here."

The expression on Trey's face made me stifle a giggle. "Who is she?" I asked.

"Just the daughter of a close friend of mine," Marti said. She gave my shoulder a squeeze. "Now come inside, and I'll introduce you to the rest of the crew."

The rest of the crew turned out to be Pringles, the African grey parrot — who about broke my eardrums with his squawking — Thomas and Thumbelina, brother and sister Siamese cats; and Lacey, the tan-and-white Chihuahua, who stalked around me with great suspicion.

"Everyone's friendly," Marti said, raising her voice over the squawking, "except for Pringles. Don't ever stick your finger in his cage, or he'll take it off."

The parrot twisted his head sideways and eyed me. "Take it off," he said, "take it off."

I jumped back. "He talks!"

"He never shuts up," Trey said.

Marti looked offended. "That's not true. He's just excited because we have company." She took my bag from me. "Come on, and I'll show you your room."

I followed her across the polished vinyl floor, around a leather sectional sofa, and into a small bedroom flooded with sunshine. She set my things on the twin bed and spread her hands. "It's not big, but it's all yours as long as you're here. Are you hungry? Do you want something to drink? I have lemonade, Dr Pepper, or there's always ice water."

I shook my head. "I'm okay, thanks."

Trey had followed us into the bedroom, and he checked his watch. "If you girls are set, I should probably go."

"Oh, TJ," Marti said. "Do you really have to leave so soon?"

"Yeah, Mom. I told the captain I'd only be a half hour." He bent to give her a quick kiss. "You two behave yourselves now, you hear?"

"We'll consider it," Marti said. "But we just may decide to create a ruckus."

It felt so weird to watch Trey walk out the door. *Wait!* I wanted to call out to him. *How long am I staying here? When can I go see Grandma Beth again?*

"Do you know how long I'm supposed to be here?" I asked.

"I don't," Marti said. "Hopefully a few days at the very least."

"Well, thanks for letting me come."

"I'm delighted you're here. You're a very important witness, Poppy. And my son likes to keep very close tabs on his witnesses, especially . . ." She cut herself off with an alarmed look and cleared her throat. "Well, let's just say, especially someone like you."

My mind darted back to my short conversation with Trey after leaving the Huckleberry Home. "Do you know Virginia Sykes?"

"Virginia Sykes," she echoed softly. "I haven't heard that name for quite a while. Did he tell you about her?"

"Yeah," I lied.

"What did he say?"

"That I looked like her and stuff. How did he know her?"

Marti worried her teeth over her bottom lip. "She was a little neighbor girl. I'm afraid I can't say too much more than that."

"Oh, okay. Sorry."

"No, no, nothing to be sorry about." She reached out and took my hand again. "You know, I've been a widow for seven years now. But before that, I was a police sergeant's wife for twenty-six years. And I learned the hard way that it doesn't pay to be a blabbermouth, even though that's still my normal tendency. Make sense?"

"Um . . . sure."

"Good, now come sit and tell me all about your grandmother. She sounds like a lovely lady."

We sat on the leather sofa, and Lacey the Chihuahua came and curled up in a tiny ball against my hip. I rubbed my knuckle along her back while I told Marti about Grandma Beth and about how I planned to get her out of the nursing home as soon as I could. She listened carefully, leaning close like what I had to say was super important. Then after a while she said, "Poppy, may I ask what happened to your parents?"

I ran my tongue over my top teeth. I hated talking about my parents, it always made me achy and sad and mad all at the same time. But Marti had been so nice to me, how could I be mean? "It's actually a pretty short story. I never knew either of them. They were both professors of botany. My grandma told me they got awarded some special grant to go to Botswana and study the plants and flowers of Africa, and then teach for a semester at a local university."

"Wow, what an impressive opportunity."

"Yeah, but I wasn't quite a year old. And they were afraid to take a baby someplace like that because they didn't know how safe it would be. So they left me with Grandma Beth. She said they called two or three times a week for the first month, but then all of a sudden the calls just stopped. A week or so later, Grandma got a call from the U.S. embassy in Africa. They told her some anti-government rebels had bombed the university."

Marti's gray eyes were huge. She drew in a long, slow breath. "And . . . your parents were killed?"

"Along with ten other people."

"Oh, Poppy. I'm so sorry."

I looked away as the familiar ache took over my stomach. This was the part of the story that always made it hurt the worst. "If they'd stayed home and taken care of me like they should have, nothing would have happened to them."

Marti drew back, and I saw the same surprise I'd seen in Trey's eyes, only Marti didn't hide it nearly as well. And I felt bad, because I wanted her to like me. But as Grandma Beth often said — truth wasn't always soft and fuzzy and warm, sometimes it was cold and hard as steel. But whether it was easy to hear or not, truth was truth.

Marti looked off into the air. "I'm seldom speechless, but I honestly don't know what to say, Poppy. I'm just so sorry for your loss." She shook her head. "So your grandmother kept you."

"Yeah, and we've done real good together. Lots of kids live with their grandparents."

Marti clicked her tongue. "And then if all that upset wasn't enough, you ended up witnessing a crime on top of it. I bet you feel like your life's turned into a salt shaker."

"Or a snow globe. I have one of those."

"You do? I'd love to see it."

I eased away from the little dog and went into the bedroom. Below my flannel blanket, the little snow globe lay nestled in my sweatshirt. I went back out to settle on the couch with Marti and held up the globe. She slipped on her glasses for a closer look. Sunshine poured through her living room window and lit up the little red barn nestled safely inside the globe. A fir tree stood behind the barn and, in front, three tiny yellow chickens circled around a farmer, his hand hidden inside a bucket of feed.

I told Marti about the day Grandma Beth had bought it for me as a reward for good behavior at a dentist's appointment, and about how she'd trailed me around the store, patiently waiting, until I finally picked the one I wanted.

"It's charming," Marti said. "I can imagine how special it must be to you."

I gave the globe a shake, and the scene turned into a flurry of white. But the blizzard quickly settled into a gentle shower of snowflakes that dropped one by one until everything was still again. Then I glanced up to find Marti watching me, and it made me feel self-conscious to have shared so much personal stuff with somebody I'd just met. I cleared my throat. "How come you call Trey 'TJ'?"

Marti smiled. "Oh, he's named after his father, Jedidiah. But Trey Jedidiah seemed like such a big name when he was little, so he became TJ. Of course, nobody calls him that anymore, except for me."

"He said you used to take in foster kids."

"Yes, quite a few over the years."

"But you don't anymore?"

"No, that's something Jedidiah and I did together. But once I lost him, everything changed."

There was that word again. *Lost.* "What happened to him?"

"He died of complications from emphysema. He smoked a lot when he was young." She shook her head sadly. "Such a dangerous, nasty habit."

The doorbell chimed. Lacey shot off my lap, and Pringles went to pieces. I covered my ears, while Marti scrambled up and hushed everyone before she opened the door.

Miss Austin stepped in carrying a canvas duffel bag and looking a little surprised by all the racket. "My, my," she said, when things quieted. "No one could sneak up on you, now could they?"

I expected Miss Austin to introduce herself, but after listening to the two of them talk for a minute, I realized they'd already met. "Would you like some coffee or lemonade?" Marti asked.

Miss Austin shook her head. "Thanks so much, but I only have a minute." She held out the canvas bag to me. "Here you are, Poppy, your homework for the next few days. Make sure you do it so you don't get behind."

I couldn't help but smile at the thought of getting to skip school for a few days. "I could get used to this."

"Well, don't. It's only until Detective Brannigan feels it's safe for you to go back."

I wondered if any of the kids would miss me. I got along okay with most of them but didn't really have a best friend, because I liked drawing a lot better than I liked hanging out. I *would* miss Luke, though. He liked to draw, too — things like robots and wizards and outer-space creatures. And he didn't do dumb stuff just to show off like most of the other boys. He was quiet and nice and really cute, too. He'd probably notice I wasn't there. At least I hoped he would.

"Do you need anything else while I'm here?" Miss Austin asked. "Oh, wait, I nearly forgot." She dug in her purse and pulled out a cell phone. "Is this yours?"

My mouth dropped open. "My phone! How did you get it?"

"I'm not sure. It was lying on my desk with a little note with your name written on it."

"No kidding?" I wondered if Trey had anything to do with it. He would've had to go directly to the center after he left me with Marti. But I didn't really care. I was just so happy to have it back.

"Anything else you need before I run?"

"Can I go home to get some more clothes and stuff? I've had the same two pair of jeans for ten days."

"Of course. I'll try to get you over there soon, promise." She rolled her eyes at Marti and reached to open the door. "It's been crazy lately. I used to have ten or twelve children on my caseload, but now it averages nineteen or twenty. I swear, sometimes I don't have time to eat."

Marti watched Miss Austin head down the steps. "Thanks for bringing Poppy's things by," she said, offering a final wave before she closed the door. Then she turned to me and put a fingertip on her chin. "From the looks of that woman, I'd say she finds plenty of time to eat."

I burst out laughing. Marti gave me a dismayed look and hid her face in her hands. "Oh, Lord, did I just say that? And here I told you I wasn't a blabbermouth." She checked her watch. "Would you do me a favor, Poppy? Take a glass of lemonade out to Lizzie?"

My grin faded. I'd forgotten all about the girl. "Uh . . . she didn't seem too friendly."

"Don't take it personally. She's really not a bad kid, just a little mixed-up right now." She gave me a reassuring smile. "You don't have to talk for an hour, just offer her some lemonade."

"Okay, then," I said.

I followed Marti into the kitchen and waited for her to fill two glasses with lemonade and ice cubes. "Okay, one for you and one for Lizzie." She pointed to a sliding door. "Here, I'll get the door for you."

I stepped out onto a wooden deck overlooking a backyard

brimming with flowers and shrubs. Lizzie knelt beside a ceramic bathtub planted with papery red poppies. I took a deep breath for courage and forced myself to walk over to her.

There was a smudge of dirt across her chin. I tried not to focus on it as I held out a glass. "Here. Marti thought you might want this."

She hesitated a second and then reached for it. "Okay."

Her shoulder-length hair and square-cut bangs made her look just like Cleopatra, but it was the pink highlights that were really impressive. "Cool hair."

She gave me an intense look, as if trying to determine if I was making fun of her. Then her face relaxed a bit. "If I could just convince my mom of that."

I wanted to leave, but the scissors and sandwich baggie in her hand got my curiosity up. "What are you doing?"

"Cutting off seed pods. Lame, huh?"

Harvey appeared at my side. I crouched down and laid my cheek against his wide head, thankful for the distraction. "Do you go to Whitmore Middle School? I've never seen you around."

Lizzie anchored her glass of lemonade against a paving stone and went back to snipping seed pods. "I used to go to the Meadow Creek charter school, but then a couple of months ago my mom got this wonderful, lame idea to homeschool me."

"How come?"

" 'Cause I'm a bad kid."

I laughed. I couldn't help it.

She gave a long-suffering sigh, and I expected her to tell me to get lost. But instead, she set the scissors down and picked up her lemonade again. "Okay, I'll do you a favor and give you the thirty-second version. I got caught spray-painting the federal building because my friend Tanya is a really lousy lookout. So me and her and my best friend, Brett, got sentenced to three hundred hours of community service."

"The *federal* building? Wow, you guys are" — I wanted to say *pretty stupid*, but caught myself in time — "pretty brave."

She smiled. "Yeah, it was awesome until we got caught."

"What did you paint on it?"

"Pete for president."

"Who's Pete?"

"Just this guy in my class that I kinda liked."

I thought about Luke again. He'd called me at home once. It was only to ask about a history assignment, but I'd still gotten nervous and laughed. But he hadn't acted upset. He'd laughed, too. "So what do you have to do for your community service?"

66

"I've been doing most of it at the animal shelter because that's where my mom works. It was better than picking up garbage on the side of the road or pulling weeds at the community garden."

"That's your punishment? Dogs are awesome."

She rolled her eyes. "They eat, poop, shed, and drool. Pretty nasty if you ask me."

I tightened a protective arm around Harvey. "Yeah, well, people do most of that stuff, too. But dogs love you no matter what. They make pretty good lookouts, too."

She smirked. "Good point."

"What do your friends have to do for their community service?"

"Tanya's mowing lawns and doing yard work. I dunno about Brett. She won't answer any of my texts. I think she hates me."

"Oh," I said. Her comment about texting made me think about my phone. I needed to check it out and make sure Sidney hadn't done anything to it. I gave Harvey a final squeeze and jumped up. "Well, I gotta go. Have fun snipping."

She seemed a little disappointed. "Yeah, whatever."

I went into the bedroom and plugged in my phone. There were the three missed calls from Grandma Beth and a bunch of calls and texts sent by Sidney. At least her fun ended when the phone went dead. Jerk.

I went out to ask Marti to help me find the number for the Huckleberry Home and then entered it into my phone. But when I tried to call Grandma Beth just to make sure the number worked, a nurse answered instead. She told me afternoon wasn't the best time to call since many of the residents napped after lunch. She said Grandma Beth had physical therapy each morning at eight-thirty and that it would be best to call after that.

"What does she do for physical therapy?" I asked.

"Mobility exercises and stretching mostly."

I wasn't sure what mobility exercises were, but it gave me an instant idea. "Are family members allowed to watch?"

"I don't see why not."

I bounced up and down on my tiptoes. "Great. Thanks. When my grandma wakes up can you please tell her I have my cell phone back?"

I ended the call with a grin. I'd just figured out a way to get Grandma Beth out of the old people's home.

Chapter Five

A LITTLE while later, I helped Marti chop cabbage and potatoes for our supper. Both dogs were flopped in the middle of the floor, smack in the way. Country music played on the radio, and Marti hummed along. It made me think of Luke again. I knew he liked country because he had a Toby Keith world tour sticker on his notebook, and a baseball cap advertising Kat Country 96. I liked that station, too, but didn't get to listen to it much because Grandma Beth preferred to listen to soft jazz. But after I went to bed each night, I'd turn my clock radio on low, and fall asleep to the velvety voice of Delilah Rayne counting down the top country songs. I wondered if Luke listened to the show. If I ever worked up the courage, I'd ask him.

Trey got home in time to eat with us. We sat around Marti's oak table, with a steaming platter of corned beef in the center and a basket of wheat rolls off to the side. I looked at the empty fourth chair and thought how perfect it would be if Grandma Beth were there. After dinner, Trey scooted back his chair and wiggled a finger at me. "Come with me," he said. "I'll give you a tour of my half of the duplex."

"Grab a sweatshirt," Marti told me. "He keeps it like an icebox over there."

Trey rolled his eyes. "Sixty-eight is not an icebox, Mom. And my electric bill's half of yours."

She gave him a defiant smile and waved her hands beside her head. "You can freeze if you want, son. I'd rather be warm."

Thumbelina batted at my shoelace as I pushed away from the table, and I had to take a quick hop to keep from tripping. I grabbed my hoodie from the bedroom and followed Trey out into the cool evening air. It smelled like barbecue, somebody's last-ditch effort to hang on to late summer. We walked down twenty feet of sidewalk to Trey's door, and he flipped on the light as we stepped in. His place had the same damp, earthy smell as his jacket.

"Hey," I said, "isn't that the same couch your mom has?"

"It was a combo deal," he said, "buy the sectional and get the sofa for free." He grabbed a beer from the refrigerator and popped the top.

I wandered over to look at a framed photo of a young couple. "Are these your parents?"

"Yep. Clear back in 1976."

The younger Marti was thinner and had light brown hair instead of white, but her face didn't look a whole lot different. "Your mom's really nice."

"Yeah. She's a big, sweet pushover."

I thought of Grandma Beth, and it made my throat feel thick. I studied the picture again. Trey's father stood unsmiling and stiff in his dark blue uniform, his suit jacket decorated with a bunch of stripes and ribbons and little metal symbols. He looked pretty scary. "What was your dad like?"

Trey laced his hands behind his neck and twisted in a stretch. "Tough. Mom thought he was too hard on me." He smiled. "I got lots of whippings when I was a kid. Most of them deserved."

Something about that made my mind jump back to Sidney. "Oh, hey, were you the one who got my phone back for me?"

Trey gave me a mysterious smile. "Oh, I might've had something to do with it."

I couldn't help but grin at all the possibilities filling my mind. "Sidney had it, didn't she? I told you. What did you do? Did you search the room? Did you put her in handcuffs?"

He chuckled. "No, no. We just had a nice, friendly chat in the director's office."

I gave him a doubtful look. I couldn't picture Sidney having a "friendly" conversation with anybody. "But what did you say?"

"You got your phone, right?"

I nodded, disappointed he wouldn't give me more details. "Yeah. Thank you."

"You're welcome." He opened a cabinet below the TV and pulled out a box of checkers. "You up for a game?"

I brightened. Grandma Beth and I played checkers all the time. "Sure. Be warned, though, I'm pretty good."

"Oh, yeah? Prove it."

He moved to the sofa and swept aside a TV remote and a Tom Clancy novel from the coffee table. I sat across from him on the rug and carefully plotted my moves. But it didn't take me long to realize I was outmatched. At least I did get to jump him twice. I even managed a double jump. Halfway through the game I went to the kitchen for a drink of water.

"Glasses are to the left of the sink," Trey said.

I opened the cabinet and stared. Above the glasses and coffee mugs, three boxes of Twinkies filled the shelf. Just looking at them made my mouth water. "How come you have all these Twinkies?"

"What's the problem?" he said. "You have something against Twinkies?"

"No, I love them."

"Have one."

I eagerly pulled down a box and opened it. "Grandma Beth won't buy them for me. She says they're just empty calories."

"Then in that case you better have two."

I laughed. "How about if I just take all three boxes over to your mom's?"

"You're not big enough to take my Twinkies."

I grinned as I peeled back the plastic wrapper and bit into the spongy sweetness of one of the little cakes. Happy Meals one day and Twinkies the next — what would Grandma Beth think? I carried my second Twinkie out to the living room to finish our game.

"My dad taught me to play checkers when I was six years old," Trey told me. "He never let me win. But on my thirteenth birthday I finally beat the old man fair and square. Proudest moment of my life."

I considered it. I wasn't sure what the proudest moment of my life was. Maybe when my drawing of a bulldog won first place in our school's art contest and there'd been an article in the *Spokesman-Review*.

"Want to play again?" I asked Trey when our game was over. But he glanced at his watch. "It's quarter to nine. You better get back over to Mom's before she thinks I kidnapped you."

I reluctantly stood. "Okay. Thanks for the checkers . . . and the Twinkies."

"Yep. See you tomorrow." He walked over and opened the door for me.

I started down the sidewalk and then turned on an afterthought. "I'm gonna walk home tomorrow morning and get my bike, okay?"

Trey's head whipped up. "Not alone you aren't."

The hair on the back of my neck prickled. "It's only a few blocks."

"Not alone, Poppy," he repeated, his voice taking on a hard edge. "I'll run you over there after work."

"You think that guy might be looking for me?"

"Not necessarily. But I'm not willing to take that chance."

I swallowed. I had to fight a sudden urge to look over my shoulder. "Oh . . . well okay, then. I guess I won't. Good night."

Trey watched until I reached Marti's door. I paused for a few seconds. It didn't seem right to just walk in, but it seemed funny to knock. I tapped the door a few times before slowly opening it. "Hey," I said, "I'm back." I expected Pringles to screech, but he was silent beneath his sheet-covered cage.

Marti looked up from the kitchen table, a pencil poking out from above her ear. "Well, there you are. Have a nice time?"

"Yeah. We played checkers and had Twinkies."

She laughed. "That sounds just like a man, now doesn't it?"

I thought about it. I didn't know very many men. I liked my science teacher, Mr. Harrison. And the pharmacist at the drugstore, Mr. Cunningham, always took time to talk with me when Grandma Beth bought her medicine. The only other man I saw pretty often was Larry, the handyman at our apartment, who always walked around in paint-spattered coveralls. None of them were anything like Trey.

"I've set some things in the bathroom for you," Marti said. "A new toothbrush and paste, and some lotion in case you need them. And since I'm a night owl, I tend to sleep late in the morning, so if you're up before me, you help yourself to breakfast. Do you like blueberry bagels? Or there's toast. Or hard-boiled eggs in the fridge. Whatever you can find. I mean it now, promise me you won't be shy."

"Okay, promise. Thank you. Good night."

I crawled into bed and pulled the covers up. The sheet smelled faintly of vanilla, and I held it close to my nose and worried over Trey's warning not to go to home by myself. It's not that I wasn't scared of the suspect, because I was. But the idea of Grandma Beth and I never being together again scared me a lot more. And if I didn't learn to help her myself, who knew how long she'd have to stay in the nursing home, or how long I'd be stuck at the center. And *anything* was better than being stuck at the center.

I wondered just how late in the morning Marti liked to sleep. Maybe I could make it to the Huckleberry Home and back before she ever missed me.

The next morning, the stink of burnt coffee that often woke me at the center was missing. I looked over toward Sidney's bed, and instead of smelly clothes and candy wrappers, I saw glowing sunshine and soft beige carpet. I didn't have to wait in line to use the toilet, or eat runny eggs for breakfast, or listen to any little kids cry. All I had to do was get to the Huckleberry Home on time.

I pushed back the covers and reached for my cell phone —
7:15. That gave me an hour and fifteen minutes before
Grandma Beth's physical therapy. I quietly dressed in jeans
and a polo shirt, and pulled my hoodie over my head. Then
I tiptoed out to the kitchen, gulped down a glass of orange
juice and half a bagel, and scribbled a note I hoped Marti
would never read.

> *Didn't want to wake you. Decided to go visit Grandma Beth*
> *for a while this morning. Don't worry, I know the way. I'll be*
> *back before long.*
>
> *— Poppy*

I propped it up against the sugar bowl, offered my bagel
crumbs to Harvey, and peeked out the front door. Trey's
Pontiac was gone. Good. I took a careful look around the
neighborhood. Things seemed peaceful and quiet . . .
almost too quiet, and a ripple of fear worked its way through
my stomach. I studied the houses across the street — their
garages and cars and boats, the shoulder-high row of ever-
green shrubs lining the sidewalk. What if the suspect from
the gas station *was* looking for me? There were so many
places he could hide. A strong urge to stay tugged me back
into the kitchen. But then I thought of Grandma Beth and

felt an even stronger urge to go. Harvey watched me from near the table, and I wished I could take him with me. But I knew I didn't dare without asking Marti, and besides, once I got my bike what would I do with him then?

I tied my hair back in a ponytail and flipped up my hood, then quietly closed the door behind me and started down the sidewalk. The smoky scent of somebody's wood stove filled my nose and made me think about winter. The last two winters had been disappointing, with endless gray days and not a single snow day off school. We were overdue for a good-sledding winter. Manito Park had a great sledding slope. A little short, but not so steep it killed you to walk back up. Grandma Beth refused to sled, but there were usually a few kids I knew from school.

The crisp, sweet notes of a chickadee made me look up to the trees as I trotted along, but I couldn't spot him through all the orange and yellow leaves.

In only a few minutes I started to recognize all the houses in the neighborhood, and it seemed weird to be staying so near to home without actually being home. I rounded the corner of West Twenty-First and South Howard, and there it was: our apartment building — its warm red bricks solid and welcoming. The bird feeder dangled empty from the lowest branch of the weeping willow, and I grabbed it off its nail as I passed.

A quick scan of the parking area told me who was home — our landlady, Mrs. Gilly, and elderly Mr. Jenkins. But not Nancy, the single mom who lived downstairs and got up at 3:00 a.m. to deliver the *Spokesman-Review*, or her teenage son who made the whole apartment throb when he practiced his drums.

I let myself in the bottom door that led up to our private staircase and unlocked the top door into our apartment. The air was stuffy and warm and still smelled of Grandma Beth's rose-scented hand lotion. I filled a quart canning jar and watered the Christmas cactus in the kitchen. Then I let the message machine play while I headed into my bedroom.

My room felt eerily quiet, lonely almost. I threw some clean clothes in my backpack and then paused to look at all my things — stuffed animals, creased comic books, the checkers board-game box with the split corners, the swim goggles I never used, the star maps and puzzle books, the familiar wallpaper with the pink and yellow balloons I'd outgrown.

Grandma's big book of famous quotations waited on my

dresser, a ragged red ribbon marking our spot two-thirds of the way through. It was getting harder to remember how many we'd missed — was it thirty-six or thirty-nine? I thought about taking the time to read just one, but it didn't seem fair to the others. I ran a finger over the book's faded black cover. "Be back soon," I whispered, "with Grandma Beth."

I grabbed my sunglasses for an extra bit of disguise, then hefted my backpack and hurried to the basement laundry, where we stored my bike and the bag of birdseed. I filled the feeder with black oil sunflower seeds and hung it back on the willow before climbing on my bike.

I decided to take the side roads to the Huckleberry Home, where the sidewalks were wider and there was less traffic. Besides, the back way took me past Manito Park, with its beautiful gardens and conservatory, where Grandma Beth and I loved to study the exotic cacti and tropical plants. The park had the best view of the stars, too, especially on warm summer nights, in the open grassy plot between the lilac gardens and the ancient stone arch.

Maybe it was because my mind was swimming with thoughts of Grandma Beth and stars and plants, but I nearly crashed my bike when I saw the poster. I fought for my balance, came to a wobbly stop, and stared. The sketch I'd helped Cindy create glared at me from a telephone pole outside the entrance to Manito Park. I took in the rough edge of the suspect's jaw and the empty look in his eyes. Seeing the sketch in the safety of the interview room was bad enough, but seeing it here, alone, made goose bumps jump along my arms.

I looked over my shoulder. A few people mingled around the food cart at the far end of the parking lot, but the park was mostly quiet at this time of morning. Trey's words rattled around in my head — *Not alone, Poppy* — and all my fear from an hour before came flooding back. I wished I hadn't ignored him. I wished he were with me now. I made sure my hair was still tucked into my hood and bumped up my sunglasses.

That's when I noticed the beat-up green van across the street.

The driver's window was halfway down, and a man peered out at me from beneath a black baseball cap. All my muscles jumped, and my heart almost splattered right out onto the pavement. It was *him*. It had to be. Why else would he be staring at me? I wanted to scream. I wanted to get off my bike and run.

Run where? The food cart? Down the sidewalk?

My legs made the decision for me, and I pushed off, pedaling as fast as I could go. The rush of wind ripped my hood back, but I was too afraid to stop and fix it. Riding bent over made my muscles scream, and after a few blocks I knew if I didn't stop to catch my breath, I'd have a heart attack.

I swerved into the lot of a Safeway grocery and raced to the front entrance, where an employee was trying to maneuver a chain of carts through the door. She gave me a funny look as I jumped off my bike and almost tripped in the process. I scouted the area, ready to bolt inside. But there was no green van — no vans at all — and nobody wearing a black baseball cap. I wiped sticky bangs from my face and commanded myself to calm down.

As my heartbeat slowed, I started to second-guess myself. Was the guy in the van really the suspect from the gas station? Or was it just somebody enjoying a few minutes at the park? But if he was enjoying the park, why was he sitting in the van? Maybe he was waiting for somebody. Had I imagined the whole thing because of the poster?

I wrapped my fingers around my cell phone. I was sure Marti would come get me if I called, but she was probably still in bed, and I wasn't more than a mile from the Huckleberry Home. I took a few more shaky breaths and scanned the cars coming in and out of the grocery store — still no green van. I forced myself to pedal back to the street.

Chapter Six

I REACHED the nursing home with ten minutes to spare, which was just enough time for my breathing to go back to normal. Then I calmly walked down the hall and plastered on a smile as I stepped into Grandma Beth's room. But I lost my smile just as fast. I couldn't believe it — she was still in bed, sound asleep. The clock on her wall showed 8:25. How come she wasn't up? I walked over and prodded her shoulder. "Grandma Beth? Wake up. It's me."

She gave a little snort, opened bleary eyes, and shifted her head toward me. "Oh. Oh, Poppy. You caught me dozing."

"You're supposed to be ready for your physical therapy. I came to watch so I can learn to help you do it."

She blinked several times, as if she was trying to make sense of what I'd said. "Well, aren't you the ambitious one. But I'm afraid there's not going to be any therapy this morning."

"Why not?"

"I've been having dizzy spells. They started last evening. It's all right if I'm still, but whenever I sit up or stand, I feel like I might topple over."

Unease stirred my stomach. "You have to tell the doctor."

"He hasn't been around yet, honey. He has a lot of residents to see."

"Well, what time is he coming?"

She closed her eyes. "That's not the way things work in this place, Poppy. It's not like having a set appointment."

"But you at least told the nurses, didn't you?"

"Yes. That's why we decided to let the therapy go this morning. They said it's probably best for me to just rest."

I tried to swallow back my disappointment. "What can I do to help?"

"You can quit fretting so much. Now grab that chair by the closet and sit beside me for a minute."

I scooted the wooden chair as close to her bed as I could. She took my hand. "Who brought you today?"

"Trey," I said, without even thinking about it. "He's out in the hall someplace."

"How are things going with his mother? Is she nice?"

"Really nice."

"She's not old and gray and past her prime like me, huh?"

I knew she was trying to make me smile, but I just couldn't. "I went home this morning, Grandma. I watered the cactus and got some clean clothes and listened to the messages. Nothing important, though, just some credit card ads."

"What is today, Poppy?"

"The sixteenth, I think."

"All right. Next week sometime I want you to take eight hundred dollars and pay Mrs. Gilly the rent. You remember where our envelope is, right?"

Next week? "Can't you pay her? You'll be out by then."

Grandma Beth met my eyes. "Priscilla Marie. You know I love you more than life itself. You know that, right?"

I nodded, afraid of what she might say next.

"All right. Now I realize this may be a bitter pill to swallow, but you need to accept the fact that I may not get out of this place."

I pulled my hand free. "What are you talking about? I'm gonna get you out of here."

Grandma sighed. "I know you like to fix things, Poppy. But this isn't something you can fix. I'm seventy-six years old. I've had a stroke, and now I'm having dizzy spells. Even if I do get well enough to go home again, things aren't going to be like they used to be."

I felt like she'd slapped me. The pressure on my chest made it hard to breathe. "Why are you saying stuff like this, Grandma? You sound like you're giving up."

"Of course I'm not giving up, honey. I just . . ." She paused, and uncertainty filled her eyes. "I just need you to think about what the reality might be."

"I don't wanna think about it."

"I know. Believe me, I know. But things are going to be okay."

I dug my fingernails into my palms. I wanted to be strong for Grandma Beth. To show her I believed what she said — that things really would be okay. But an awful burning filled my nose anyway.

"Oh, Poppy," she said. "Please don't cry. You and I have always figured things out before, and we'll figure this out, too." She reached to her bedside tray and tugged a tissue from the box. "Here's an idea. How about if I let you know as soon as these dizzy spells pass, and then you can come watch my physical therapy if you like."

I wiped my nose with the tissue and forced myself to nod. My cell phone vibrated. I reluctantly sat up and pulled it from my pocket. I didn't recognize the number. "Hello?"

"Oh, Poppy! It's Marti. Where are you?" She sounded frantic.

I sat back from the bed. So much for Marti sleeping until I got back. I tried to clear the thick, sticky feeling from my throat. "I'm fine. I'm just visiting Grandma Beth."

"But not by yourself! You know you weren't supposed to take off alone. TJ said he told you that last night."

I closed my eyes. Great, Trey knew, too.

"I didn't have your cell number," Marti continued, "and TJ didn't, either. He had to get it from Miss Austin."

"Oh, sorry, I didn't think about that. But you were still asleep, and I needed to be here by eight-thirty for Grandma's physical therapy."

Marti let out a big breath. "Well, I'm just thankful you're all right. TJ's on his way to pick you up."

I hesitated. Grandma Beth was already watching me with eagle eyes, and I didn't know how to answer without digging myself in even deeper. "Yeah, okay," I finally said.

There was a pause. "Poppy," Marti asked, the doubt clear in her voice, "your grandma doesn't know you came by yourself, does she?"

"Um . . . no."

Marti gave an exasperated sigh. "All right. Well, promise me you'll wait there for TJ. Don't go anywhere."

"I will." I wanted to apologize, but I needed to get off the phone before I started laughing and made Grandma

Beth even more suspicious than she already was. "See you pretty soon."

I stuck the phone back in my pocket, hoping Marti didn't think I'd hung up on her. I faked a smile at Grandma Beth. "That was Trey's mom. She didn't know I was here because she was still sleeping this morning."

"You be sure and cooperate with her, Poppy. She's doing you a big favor by letting you stay there."

"I know," I said. I put my head near hers again. "But I feel like I should be here with you."

She patted my back. "I can't imagine why you'd want to stay."

"I miss home," I said. "I miss you."

"Not half as much as I miss you. How about after I get feeling a bit better you come and eat lunch with me in the dining room. Would you like to do that?"

I nodded. It felt so right for us to be here together, talking and planning like we'd always done. But I knew it wouldn't take Trey long to get here, and I wasn't sure what he'd say when he showed up. I kissed Grandma Beth's cheek and stood. "Can you call me? I never know the right time to call here."

She winked. "I'll do that. Now go find something better to do than hang out around an old folks' home. I love you."

I wiggled my fingers. "Love you, too. Don't forget to call me."

There was no sign of Trey in the lobby. I stood near the entryway, feeling awkward, not sure if I should stay inside or go out. I could feel the lady at the front desk eyeing me. "Could I help you with something?" she finally asked.

"Uh, no, thanks. I was just waiting for my ride." I pushed through the front door and sat on the grass next to my bike. A white Huckleberry Home bus pulled into the circle driveway. I watched the driver lower an electric wheelchair ramp and unload an old man with spindly legs and a hunched back. He left the old man sitting there while he unloaded a woman with bluish-gray hair and bright white running shoes. It seemed strange to see brand-new athletic shoes on someone who couldn't even walk. It wasn't fair.

An aide came from inside, and she and the driver wheeled the residents past. I busied myself flicking grass blades back and forth so I didn't have to meet their eyes. Grandma Beth wasn't like those people. She wasn't worn out and helpless-looking. Up until just a couple of weeks ago, we'd walked three blocks to the Handy Mart for groceries every week. She'd carried lawn chairs up and down the steps to our apartment. She'd stood at the kitchen sink each evening and washed dishes. She'd done whatever needed doing. And if she couldn't do something on her own, we figured out how to do it together. She'd said we'd figure this out, too. But I knew she was just trying to make me feel better. Because this wasn't any old easy-to-fix problem; this was a really tough one.

Trey's black car coasted up behind the bus, and I scrambled to my feet as he climbed out. His relieved expression lasted about half a second before dissolving into a hard look that made me want to run back inside to Grandma Beth.

"Hey," I said.

He strode over and took hold of my bike. "Get in the car, Poppy."

I hovered in place as he lifted my bike into the trunk and strapped it down with a bungee cord. Sweat tickled my underarms, and I started to laugh before I could stop myself.

Trey stared me into silence and jerked his thumb at the car. "Get in."

I pinched my lips together and climbed into the front seat. Trey slid behind the wheel and shut his door.

"Sorry," I said. "I didn't mean to laugh."

He turned to face me. "Did you hear me last night?"

His dark eyes drilled into me, and it suddenly felt like we were way too close together. "Yeah."

"Did you think I was joking?"

"No."

"You just figured you knew better?"

"No. I just needed to be here to watch my grandma's physical therapy, and I didn't want to wake your mom up. I wasn't trying to upset anybody."

Trey rubbed a hand across his forehead. "Yeah? Well, whatever your reason, Poppy, you took a really dangerous chance."

Heat filled my nose at the same second the tears filled my eyes. I turned up my hands. "You don't understand, Trey. Grandma Beth's the only person I've got, and I'm the only one she's got. Nobody else is worried about getting her home — only me. All you have to worry about is your stupid case."

His body stiffened. He gripped the steering wheel with an intensity that turned his knuckles white. I'm not sure where I'd gotten my burst of courage, but it shriveled right out of me, and I tried to melt into the door. "Sorry," I said quickly. "I didn't mean that last part . . . about your case."

Trey's flush of anger seemed to disappear just as fast. He relaxed his hands and shifted the car into gear. "Put on your seat belt."

We pulled up beside the duplex a few minutes later. Harvey barked, and Marti came out to the car and gave me a hug. It was a hundred times better than being alone with Trey.

"I didn't hang up on you," I told her.

"I never thought you did."

Trey released the bungee cord, and I waited for him to give me my bike. But he didn't. He kept a hold of it and wheeled it up next to Marti's front steps. Then he disappeared inside, and reappeared a few seconds later with a bike chain. I tapped a knuckle against my lip as Trey threaded the chain through the spokes of the front wheel and locked it around one of the fence posts.

I glanced at Marti and then back at Trey. "W-w-what are you doing? You can't take my bike away."

Trey pocketed the key. "Guess again," he said.

Marti laid a hand on my shoulder. "TJ," she said softly.

Trey stepped back over to us. "I'm not playing around, Poppy. Until I know you're not in danger, you're either here with Mom, or you're with me. Understand?"

I blinked fast. I wanted to ask what gave him the right. Who made him boss of me. But my tongue felt like a jumbled mess in my mouth. "How come I'm the one who gets treated like a criminal?" I blurted. "I thought I was supposed to be the valuable witness."

He raised his eyebrows. "You *are* a valuable witness. But running off half-cocked like you did was stupid."

Grandma Beth never called me stupid, she called me impulsive. But maybe they were one and the same. I backed away from Marti and stumbled indoors right before the tears came. As soon as I flopped across the bed, Lacey hopped up beside me and started licking my nose. I curled around her tiny body and cried into her fur. I cried because Grandma Beth was too sick for her physical therapy, and because I really had no idea how to get her out of the Huckleberry Home. But mostly I cried because I felt like I was free-falling with no bottom in sight.

Chapter Seven

MARTI padded down the hall and tapped on the open door. "Can I come in?"

I shrugged.

She came over and sat on the edge of the bed, and Lacey repositioned herself with a little snarl of complaint. "Don't be mad at TJ, honey. It's his job to keep you safe."

My chin trembled. "But I'm trying to do my job, too. To take care of my grandma."

"Don't you think she's being taken care of at the Huckleberry Home?"

"I dunno. I guess. But I should be the one doing it."

"Wow," Marti said softly, "your grandma sure is lucky to have such a responsible, loyal granddaughter as you. But let me ask you something. How do you think she feels knowing there's a wanted criminal out there running free who's seen you and knows your name?"

Her voice was calm and low, but the words gave me a jolt anyway. She raised her eyebrows at me. "I know you're very worried about your grandma, Poppy. But you need to worry about yourself a little, too. Taking off like you did was very risky."

I swallowed. I *was* plenty worried about myself — worried I'd never get back home and that things would never go back to normal. But I knew that's not what Marti meant. "I saw a man this morning, Marti. He was sitting in a van at Manito Park, watching me."

She tensed. "And? Did you recognize him?"

I shook my head. "Not really. It just scared me is all. I never saw him again after that."

Marti let out a slow breath. "It may have been nothing, but you'll need to tell TJ. In the meantime, I want you to promise me that you won't pull any more disappearing acts."

"Okay."

"No, I'd like to hear you say it."

"I promise."

"Good. Thank you." She winked at me and checked her watch. "Now how would you like to get your mind on something else for a while and go to the animal shelter with me?"

I perked up. "The animal shelter?"

"Remember Lizzie? Her mom, Carol, is the director, and I'm her assistant. I've got quite a bit of data entry to catch up on, and you can be a volunteer dog walker if you're game."

Lizzie. I remembered the disappointed look on her face when I'd walked off yesterday. I'd been too focused on other things to give it much thought at the time, but now I felt kind of bad for abandoning her right after she told me her best friend hated her. "Did you know Lizzie doesn't like dogs?" I asked.

Marti waved her hand in the air. "She doesn't like a lot of things, I'm afraid. But she's really not a bad kid. She's just made some pretty questionable choices lately."

"Hmm," I said. But I couldn't help thinking that maybe Lizzie was just impulsive like me. It would give us at least one thing in common. "Sure," I said. "Let's go."

A few minutes later Marti and I headed across town in her red Subaru. Not her first choice in comfort, she explained, but it handled Washington winters very well.

I was thinking about Lizzie, wondering if she'd be happy to see me or not, when Marti braked for a red light. A sketch of the suspect stared back at me from the light pole and made me shiver. A block later there was one on the front window of the Mountain West Bank, and then another on the front door of the Spokane Civic Theatre. "Guess Trey wasn't kidding," I said.

Marti glanced over. "About?"

"About plastering that guy's face all over."

She nodded. "Those sketches are a pretty useful tool. It's a great way to get the community involved in helping track a suspect down."

A few minutes later we coasted to a stop in front of a large, brown brick building. SPOKANE ANIMAL SHELTER was spelled out with big metal letters across the front.

Marti led me through the double glass doors into a small lobby that smelled of urine and bleach and some type of spearmint room freshener. Off to the right side of the greeting counter, a bunch of cats dozed or played on a carpeted tree-shaped tower.

We walked through another door into the back area, where large kennels lined both sides of a narrow, concrete walkway. A chorus of barks and howls filled the air. Hairy, hopeful faces peered out of each kennel. Most of the dogs wagged their tails, but some just stood and stared, like they didn't want to get their hopes up.

I understood the look in those eyes. I'd been feeling it ever since Grandma Beth's stroke. "Hi, guys," I crooned, my voice lost in the racket. "Good dogs."

At the end of the row a woman crouched in front of a sleepy-looking Saint Bernard. Lizzie knelt beside her, holding a metal tray with cotton swabs and peroxide, her face hidden behind her black-and-pink hair.

"Hey," the woman called when she caught sight of us, "more crazy people willing to brave the labyrinth."

Marti laughed. "Hello to you, too, Carol. I brought someone with me — Poppy Parker."

Carol smiled warmly at me. "Welcome, Poppy. I've heard a lot about you. I'd shake your hand, but I need to wash first. I hear you've already met Eliza May."

Lizzie didn't smile, but she gave me a nod that seemed friendly enough.

Carol pointed to the huge dog at her feet. "And this is Sarge. He just had paw surgery a few hours ago."

Sarge turned droopy brown eyes up to me without lifting his great head.

"Is he okay?" I asked.

"He's doing good. Just a little out of it from the anesthetic still. He'll be up for adoption as soon as he gets his stitches out next week."

She closed Sarge's kennel and motioned us through a swinging door at the end of the hall. We stepped out into an office area and the noise level dropped way down.

"It's not always that bad," Carol said. "They just get excited when someone walks through."

"It is *too* always that bad," Lizzie said. "I'm gonna finish my movie now."

"Oh, no, you're not," Carol said. "Not yet. I still have six dogs that need a walk and a bathroom break."

Lizzie rolled her eyes. "Mom, jeez!"

Carol put up a hand. "Don't even start. Judge's orders, remember, not mine." She smiled at me. "But maybe Poppy would be willing to walk some dogs with you."

I gave Lizzie a sideways glance. "Uh . . . yeah, sure."

Lizzie brushed past me with a huff, and I wasn't sure if she was mad at me, or the fact that she couldn't go back to her movie. I followed her back toward the kennels. She stopped in front of a small black poodle mix and unlatched the door. She scooped up the dog and thrust her into my arms. "Here, hold Lilly." She moved to the next kennel, pulled a leash from her pocket, and snapped it on the Rottweiler inside. "Come on, Zeus, you big ugly butt."

I trailed Lizzie out to a grassy, fenced area behind the shelter. She nudged Zeus through the gate and gestured to me. "Put her in here."

I set the little dog inside, and Lizzie clanged the gate shut.

Then she walked over to a nearby oak tree and plopped down underneath it.

"That's it?" I said. "I thought we were supposed to walk them."

Lizzie shrugged. "They can walk themselves. They've got plenty of space."

Zeus peed on a clump of weeds near the gate and then happily trotted off. But Lilly stared at me with shining black eyes, her stub tail wagging furiously. "I think she wants somebody to play with her," I said.

Lizzie dug a cell phone from her pocket and started to text. I glanced uncertainly between her and the enclosure before I opened the gate and slipped inside. "You wanna play?" I asked the little dog. "Come on, I'll play with you." I clapped my hands as I walked through the dandelions, and she jumped around me doing twirls and leaps.

After a while I glanced over at Lizzie. She'd been a lot more talkative at Marti's. I thought again of how I'd walked off on her that day. "Hear anything from your friends?" I asked.

She looked over and shrugged. "Not much."

"Well, maybe they're too busy trying to pay off their own debt to society." I meant it to be funny, but Lizzie didn't look like she appreciated it much.

"How long will it take to do your three hundred hours?" I asked.

She shrugged again. "I dunno. Mom's keeping track. I think I've done a third of it or something."

I puffed out a quiet breath. Trying to talk to Lizzie was next to impossible. "So, when are we supposed to trade dogs?" I asked, trying to keep the irritation out of my voice.

"Whenever," she said, but she got up and came over to get Zeus. We took them back to their kennels and got out the next two — Pepper, an Australian shepherd mix, and Smokey, a purebred husky. Lizzie plopped down under the tree again. I went back in with the dogs. I snapped a few pictures of them and then tossed a tennis ball I'd found in Smokey's kennel. Both dogs tore after it, delighted.

It wasn't until we were headed back inside with Pepper and Smokey that I noticed the double kennel at the far end of the building. Inside, a large German shepherd paced back and forth, his muscles taut and his tail hung low. He trotted with a purpose, waiting until the last second to turn, as if he had someplace important to go but no way to get there. "How come that dog's by himself?"

Lizzie glanced over. "Oh, that's death row over there."

I felt a jab to my stomach. "What are you talking about?"

"It means he can't be adopted, so he's gonna be put down."

"Why can't he be adopted?"

"I dunno. You'd have to ask my mom."

I handed her Smokey's leash. "Here, put him back, will you? I wanna get a closer look."

"Whatever. Don't get bit."

I slowly approached the lone kennel. As soon as he spotted me, the dog stopped pacing and stood as still as a statue, head high, ears pricked forward. "Hey, boy," I said softly. "Hey there."

He let me get about ten feet from him before letting loose with a low, throaty growl. He had the most intelligent eyes I'd ever seen on a dog, but I forced myself to look away so he wouldn't feel challenged. "Hey there. You're a gorgeous guy, aren't you? Take it easy, boy."

I waited almost a minute, then edged closer until the low growl sounded again. "How come you're all by yourself? What did you do that was so terrible?"

I could feel him sizing me up, watching every move. I glanced up. "It's okay, boy. I won't come any closer if you don't want me to. Good dog."

I was only a couple feet from the kennel when someone shouted my name. I turned, startled, and the dog jumped forward with a bark. Carol stood at the back door to the shelter, her hands on her hips. "Come away from there, Poppy. You can't trust him."

I didn't want to end our first encounter like this, but Carol was heading my way, and I knew there wasn't a choice. I walked toward her. "He's okay," I said, "he just doesn't know me."

"He's not okay. He's unpredictable. That's why he's out here instead of with the other dogs."

"Unpredictable how?"

"Well, the man that turned him in said he bit his nine-year-old son. And then he nipped one of the other dogs the first day he was here."

"Where did he come from before that?"

"I don't know much, unfortunately. But his name is Gunner, and from what I've been able to piece together he's been bounced around to several different homes. Could be why he's aggressive. He doesn't know who to trust."

"Lizzie said you might put him to sleep."

Carol sighed. "I can't in good conscience adopt him out."

"Maybe it wasn't his fault. Maybe the kid he bit had it coming."

Carol gave me a small, sad smile. "Possibly. But it's not a chance I can take."

Gunner watched us, ears pointed forward, listening. It made me sick to stand there and talk about such a thing in front of him. "Do you . . . do it yourself?" I whispered.

"What, the euthanasia? No, we have a local vet who takes care of it for us."

"But he's so beautiful. Look at the way he holds himself."

Carol looked over at Gunner, and her shoulders slumped. "I know, kiddo. That's why he's still here. But I need to quit delaying the inevitable. Anyway, he's off limits, understand?" She gave me a playful nudge. "If you get hurt, you won't come back, and I need all the volunteers I can get."

"I'll come any time Marti will bring me."

"That won't present much of a problem. She's been babbling about you nonstop ever since she found out Trey was bringing you home."

"You know Trey?"

"I do. Marti and I have been friends for years." She dipped her chin. "Plus I've gotten better acquainted with several of our law enforcement officers thanks to some antics Eliza May pulled a few months back."

"Yeah, she mentioned that the other day."

Carol's shoulders jumped back. "Are you serious? You got lemon puss to talk! Holy smokes, I'm impressed."

I grinned. "She just gave me the bare details."

"Hey, that's more than she's been giving me lately. Whatever you did, please keep doing it."

Two pit bull mixes came bounding out the back door, dragging Lizzie behind, and I went to help her. As soon as we got them to the enclosure she went back to texting beneath the oak. I roamed around with the dogs for a while and then sat down inside the fence. One of the pit bulls came and laid his head in my lap, his tongue lolling back and forth like he was laughing. I took several pictures of him so I could maybe draw him later and then stroked his face while I watched Gunner.

He'd gone back to pacing, but he stopped about every tenth lap to stare over toward me — almost like he wanted me to come back, like he had something important he needed to say — before it was too late.

Chapter Eight

THAT evening while Marti watched TV, I sat beside her on the couch and thumbed through my art pad. It was full of dog sketches. Someday I'd have my own dog again, but in the meantime, drawing them was better than nothing. I found an empty page near the back and started to sketch Gunner. I erased and restarted several times until I'd come as close as I could to capturing his intense chocolate eyes, and the slope of his hips, and the noble way he held his head. Then I drew a lilac bush next to him, like the ones in Manito Park, where Grandma Beth and I liked to sit in the summertime.

"Am I ever going to be allowed to see?" Marti asked.

I glanced up, surprised. "What time is it?"

"Nine o'clock. You worked through an entire episode of Sherlock Holmes."

I took a final glance at my sketch. I didn't like people watching me draw, but I didn't mind sharing my art once it was as good as I could make it. I turned my art pad to face Marti.

Her eyes lit up. "My gosh, Poppy. That's wonderful. I had no idea you could draw like that."

My chest felt lighter. "Thanks. But animals are the only things I'm good at. My people look like stick figures."

"Somehow I doubt that." She reached for my art pad and took a closer look. "You have absolutely captured Gunner. I am so impressed. You really like him, don't you?"

"You can't let Carol put him to sleep."

Marti fingered the jeweled chain around her neck. "I'm afraid I don't have any say over that, hon. But I can assure you that Carol's as big an animal lover as they come. She'd never put down any dog if there was another option."

"But he's not mean, Marti. He almost let me walk right up to him, at least until Carol scared him and ruined everything."

Marti clucked her tongue. "And you shouldn't have walked up to him to begin with." She handed my sketch pad back to me. "Things would certainly be simpler if he hadn't bitten that boy."

"The kid probably teased him, or scared him, or something.

Or else, maybe Gunner's kind of impulsive like me, and he just didn't think it through enough."

Marti smiled. "Maybe so," she said. "It's tough when you don't know the whole story. But if we adopt out a dog with an aggressive history and someone else gets hurt, it could cause legal problems for the shelter. All the animals could end up suffering. Does that make sense?"

"I guess," I said. "But even if he didn't have a good reason for biting that kid, he shouldn't have to pay with his life. That'd be kind of like Lizzie getting the death penalty for spray-painting the federal building."

Marti's eyes got really big, and her hand flew to her mouth to cover her grin. "Oh, Poppy," she said.

I hadn't been trying to be funny, but her expression made me giggle anyway. "Well, it's true," I said. I closed my art pad and put my pencils away. "How come Trey doesn't like her working over here?"

"Oh, well, as you've probably noticed, she has quite an attitude sometimes, and he has zero tolerance for mouthy kids."

I grinned. "Lizzie, mouthy? Really?"

Marti wiggled her eyebrows. "She tries to come across as so tough, but she honestly can be a sweet girl. You know what she's really good at?"

I shook my head.

"Anything to do with hair. She cuts her mom's hair, and she's even done mine. And when Carol's hair used to be longer, Lizzie would do the best French braids for her. And even though she went a little crazy with the pink highlights, they actually look very professional, don't you think?" Marti put her fingertips against her mouth. "But please don't tell her I said that. I'd get in big trouble with Carol."

I laughed. "Okay." I looked over at the clock. It was after nine, and Grandma Beth hadn't called, which meant she probably wasn't feeling good. The worry of it all made me sleepy.

Marti must have read my mind, because she reached over and gave my hand a squeeze. "Lizzie's coming over to work in the morning again, but if your grandma's feeling up to a visit by the afternoon, I'll drive you there. Sound good?"

Her hand was warm, and it sent a ribbon of warmth up my arm and around my heart. I squeezed her hand back. Being here at her house didn't feel so weird anymore. It was starting to feel pretty good.

A nurse from the Huckleberry Home called the next morning. She told me Grandma Beth was on a new medicine that thinned her blood and made her sleep most of the time, and that it would probably be best to put off a visit for a day or two. She'd be sure to let me know when there was a change.

Marti made me a fried-egg sandwich for breakfast and told me not to worry. Then she sent me out to sit in the sun on the back porch and work on homework. I was drawing little doodles in the margin of my math assignment, thinking about everything except math, when Lizzie walked into the backyard.

"Hey," she said.

I sat up. "Oh, hey."

She wore washed-out blue jeans and a black sweatshirt with a bright pink peace symbol that matched her highlights. Marti brought her a pair of garden gloves and a shovel and showed her the two flower beds that needed weeding.

I watched her pull weeds for a while, before deciding that anything was better than homework. "So, when do you do homeschool?" I asked.

She glanced over. "It just depends on what's going on. Usually afternoon or evening. It only takes about three hours a day."

"Wow, I wish regular school only took three hours."

"Seems longer when you're stuck doing it alone, though."

I closed my math book. "Need any help pulling weeds?" I asked.

She gave me a comical look. "You must be bored to death."

"I am."

She scratched her nose with the back of her wrist. "Why exactly are you here anyway?"

It wasn't really what I wanted to talk about, but at least she *was* talking. "I'm just staying with Marti for a few days." I set my math book aside and ambled over to sit on the railroad tie of the bed she was working on. "Actually, it's because I witnessed a crime, and Trey brought me here instead of taking me back to the kids' center."

Lizzie's eyes flew open. "What crime?"

"An armed robbery."

"No way! Did you see somebody get shot?"

I saw the face of the cashier, and my stomach tightened. "No, not exactly." I pulled a weed from the soil and tossed it in Lizzie's black bucket. "But I *heard* someone get shot, and then I saw the guy who did it."

"No way. Did he see you?"

I nodded, which wasn't quite as scary as saying it out loud.

"Then Trey probably thinks the guy is looking for you."

"Maybe."

"That guy hates me."

I looked up, confused. "Who hates you?"

"Trey."

I decided she was awfully quick to assume people hated her, but then I remembered Trey's stony expression the day I'd first met her and what Marti had just told me last evening.

"How long have you known him?"

"Mom and Marti have been friends for a long time. He's figured me for a troublemaker from day one. But then that night, when me and Brett and Tanya got hauled in for painting the federal building — who do you think I got the privilege of talking to?"

"Trey?"

She rolled her eyes. "Good guess. Now he's just another on a long list of people who think I'm on the road to self-destruction."

I laughed. "You'd make a great dramatic actor."

"Yeah, well, sometimes I wish my life *was* a movie. It'd be rated R, of course. How about yours?"

"How about my what?"

She sighed. "You're a little slow on the uptake, aren't you? Your life. If it was a movie, what would it be rated?"

I thought about it. "Uh, well . . . up till a few days ago I'd probably say G. But now, it'd be more like PG-13."

The sliding sound of the screen door made both of us look up. Marti stepped out onto the back porch. She looked at my homework lying at her feet and then smiled out at us. "You know the interesting thing about homework?"

I shook my head.

"It doesn't do itself," she said.

"Oh, right." I gave Lizzie an apologetic look. "Guess I can't help anymore."

"You were helping?"

"I dropped one weed in the bucket."

"Hey," she whispered as I stood. "You text?"

"Sure, why?"

She gave me another one of those slow-on-the-uptake looks, but it wasn't unfriendly. "We can keep talking and nobody will hear, duh."

I smiled. "Oh. What a rebel. You really are on the road to self-destruction."

She had a light, airy laugh that was easy to listen to, and I caught Marti's look of utter amazement before she turned and went back inside.

I managed to finish my math, even with my phone buzzing every couple of minutes. But then Lizzie left after lunch, and without being able to visit Grandma Beth, the rest of the day stretched out before me, long and empty. The sun had moved to the other side of the house by then, so I took my sketch pad out to Marti's front steps. Harvey sprawled on the lawn, snoring loudly, his stubby front legs resting perfectly on top of each other like wooden blocks. Then he started to twitch and snort, and I wondered what he was dreaming of.

I didn't remember leaning my head against Marti's iron railing, or closing my eyes. All I remembered was starting to sketch Harvey, but his deep bark suddenly scared me half to death. I jerked up to see Trey's Pontiac come to a stop against the curb. My pencil lay two steps below on the lawn, and a little string of drool ran from the corner of my mouth. I wiped it away, disgusted, as Trey climbed out of the car.

"Hey," he called. "Just the person I wanted to see."

That woke me up fast. I'd barely said ten words to him since he'd taken my bike away. "Me?" I echoed dumbly.

"Yeah, you," he said. "Come on over to my place for a minute, I've got good news."

I slowly stood and set my sketch pad on the top step. The drawing of Harvey was only half done. I followed Trey inside his apartment and stopped near his desk. "What?"

"The drawing you helped Cindy with is turning up all kinds of leads. We think we've got the suspect's name."

"Really?"

"Really. You did it, Tiger. High-five."

I reached up and slapped his hand, but I had no idea what to say. "How did you find out?"

"A custodian from Costco recognized him. Said he's a regular."

"What's his name?"

"William Eugene Frank. He's thirty-seven years old. Wanted on two felony warrants in Oregon."

"Felony? Is that the serious stuff or the not-so-serious?"

Trey looked like he wanted to laugh for a second. "The serious stuff. In this case, robbery and assault."

I hugged my arms around me. "So, it's him for sure?"

"We've got officers scanning the store's surveillance images right now," he said. "As soon as they find pictures of him, we're counting on you to give us a positive ID."

"Oh. And then what happens . . . if I can?"

"Then our chance of apprehending him gets a lot better."

I wanted to force the discussion one step further, to ask the same question again — *And then what happens?* But I didn't need to ask. I already knew the answer, and it gave me a sick feeling in the pit of my stomach. Once an arrest was made, I wouldn't be needed anymore. My job would be done, and I'd get shipped back to the center. My knees turned watery, and I leaned against Trey's desk.

116

His cell phone vibrated and made me jump. I recognized Captain Ross's voice on the other end. Trey listened for a minute and then patted the chest pocket of his shirt in search of something. He opened a desk drawer and grabbed a pen.

I glanced into the drawer. The key to the bike chain lay on top, but it was the photo lying next to it that captured my attention. It was a school picture of a young girl, her dark hair in ponytails, her lips shiny with gloss. I took it out for a closer look. Her eyes were brown, and her lips fuller than mine, but other than that it could have been me a year or two ago. It was weird. I turned the picture over. *To Trey, Love Virginia. 5th grade.*

I was so intrigued with the picture that it took a minute to realize Trey's phone call had ended. I glanced up to find him watching me. I giggled and tossed the picture back in the drawer. "Sorry. I was just . . ."

"Told you she looked like you."

"Yeah, she kind of does."

Silence hung in the air. Trey reached over and closed the drawer. I took a step back, feeling like I'd done something wrong.

"They'll have the surveillance images ready by morning," he said. "I'll be over to get you."

"Okay," I said, grateful for the easy out. "See you then."

I lay awake for a long time that night, clutching my flannel blanket, my mind whirling too fast for sleep. *William Eugene Frank — William Eugene Frank*, my mind chanted the name over and over, trying to make it fit the man with the fake-looking eyes and the awful breath. But it didn't fit. It sounded more like the name of a banker, or a lawyer maybe, or a college professor. It wasn't a criminal-sounding name. But mostly I thought about what would happen once I identified him.

Getting to stay here with Marti was a completely lucky break that I'd hoped might last until Grandma Beth got to come home. Once she moved to the Huckleberry Home, I expected she'd only have to stay a few days, a week at most. But now I wasn't so sure. I kept seeing the bluish color of her face and thinking how she couldn't even stay awake long enough for a visit. And for the first time, I let myself imagine what that might really mean.

What if she *didn't* get better? What if she turned into one of those old, helpless people, like the woman with the bright white running shoes? Or the man with the spindly legs? What would happen to her, and to our apartment?

What would happen to me?

The thought of having to live at the center until I was grown up made me feel like someone was sitting on my chest. I'd hated every minute of the ten days I'd been there — Sidney. Lukewarm showers. Crying kids. The heavy cloud of unhappiness that hung over the place — six years would be impossible. I was suddenly too hot for the covers, and I kicked them off. But only a minute later I started to shiver and pulled them back on.

Living on my own would be better. *Anything* would be better. I wondered how long I could get away with hiding out at our apartment? If I stayed inside and didn't turn on the lights or flush the toilet, maybe no one would realize I was there. But as soon as the thought entered my mind I knew it was stupid. Mrs. Gilly had a key. She'd come up to check the plants and discover me. And what about school? What about visiting Grandma Beth?

A shaft of moonlight glowed through the window blinds, and I crept over and peered out. All I could see at this angle was a narrow strip of sky and a single twinkling star. Something about that one little star all by its lonesome made me want to cry. I wondered if Grandma Beth could see any stars from her window at the Huckleberry Home. Had she ever looked? Would we ever get to look at them together again? My throat was so thick I couldn't even swallow. I rested my forehead against the cold glass, and the tears came.

Marti shook me gently awake the next morning at seven. The surveillance images were ready, and Trey was waiting to take me. My eyelids felt gritty, like I'd never slept, and my stomach hurt. Marti insisted I drink some orange juice and eat a hard-boiled egg, and she promised me everything would be fine.

This time there were no long, boring hours spent waiting at the police station. Trey took me directly to the interview room, where two officers stood around a computer with a camera plugged in. The room smelled like old coffee and stale air. I hoped that Maria might be there, just to see a friendly face, but she wasn't. The men fanned out of the way as Trey set one of the velvet-padded chairs in front of the computer and motioned me to sit. "Okay, Poppy, tell us if you recognize anybody."

Grainy color images of the Costco store filled the monitor. The camera showed four different areas of the warehouse at the same time — sporting goods, automotive, the pharmacy, groceries — and none of the pictures were very big. I studied the people pushing carts down the aisles or waiting in line at the checkout stand, praying I didn't recognize anyone.

Nobody spoke, but I could feel Trey and the other officers hovering behind me, holding their breath, hoping. It made my palms sticky, and I wrapped my feet around the legs of the chair. "I can't really tell," I said. "Most of the people have their head down."

Trey slowly clicked through the images. "No hurry, take your time."

After about a half hour, I started to relax just a little. None of the customers looked familiar. Maybe the employee at Costco had made a mistake. But then without warning an image jumped out at me. The frame on the bottom left showed a man looking almost directly at the camera. I studied his eyes and the scraggly mustache, and I knew without a doubt it was William Eugene Frank.

Sweat trickled between my shoulder blades as I shifted my gaze to the other photos and tried not to react. If I identified him, how long would it be before he got arrested? Hours — a day — a week? How soon would they send me back to the center?

But how could I *not* identify him? He'd killed somebody — a little girl's mom. I knew what it was like to grow up without parents, and how awful it felt to never have anybody specific to blame for the loss. I saw the smiling face of the cashier, the way she'd said, "It's on me today," and I hated myself for what I was thinking. My heart thumped in my ears as I wrestled with myself.

I eased back in my chair. "No. You can . . . keep going."

"Be sure, Tiger. Take as long as you need."

Tiger. Why did he have to call me that right then? It made me hate myself even more. I pinned my elbows to my sides and leaned away from Trey. "I'm sure," I said. "It's not him."

Trey didn't respond, but I felt his disappointment and heard the slight puff of air as he sighed.

I looked at the rest of the images, but there weren't any more of William Eugene Frank. Finally Trey turned the camera off and stepped back. "That's it for now, guys. Appreciate all your hard work. Go home and get some rest."

I stared at my hands and held my stomach muscles tight as the officers filed out. Trey put a hand on the top of my head. "Come on, I'll take you back to Mom's."

My ankles hurt from being forced up against the legs of the chair, and my cheeks burned. I stood up without looking at Trey. "Sorry."

"Hey, you did fine," he said. "You earned yourself a Twinkie."

I forced a quick smile, but what I really felt like doing was throwing up. Because I hadn't done fine at all. In fact, I could hardly believe what I'd done.

Chapter Nine

I T WAS only ten o'clock when we left the police station, but it felt like so much later. A ray of sun broke through the clouds and warmed the side window of Trey's car. I tipped my head against the glass and tried to endure the awful guilt that stung like a whip.

"Have you been doing your homework?" Trey asked, pulling me from my thoughts.

"Some."

He started to say something more, but then his phone vibrated. I closed my eyes. Saved by the cell.

"Hey, Mom," Trey said. "What's up? Yeah, I'm bringing her back now. . . . Oh, shoot! When?"

I sat up, instantly alert.

"Okay," Trey said, "we'll meet you there."

"What's wrong?" I cried. "Is it Grandma Beth?"

He nodded. "Afraid so. They've moved her back to the hospital."

My stomach cramped and made me gasp. "But why? What happened?"

"I'm not sure, Tiger. Let's go find out."

My heart was in my throat for the ten minutes it took to get to the hospital. Figuring out where Grandma was and riding the elevator to the sixth floor felt even longer. Miss Austin and Marti both waited in the intensive-care family room.

"What's going on?" I asked as I ran in. "Where's Grandma Beth?"

Marti started toward me, but then held back as Miss Austin reached me first. "Your grandma's being cared for, Poppy. She had another stroke early this morning. I'm so sorry."

I couldn't believe it. My hands started flapping around like they were separate from me. This whole thing was my fault — God was punishing me for lying to the police. "Where is she? I want to see her."

Miss Austin put a hand around my wrist. "Not right yet, honey. She's still with the doctors."

I shook her free. "Leave me alone. I need to see her now."

I whirled for the door, even though I had no idea which way to go.

Trey reached out and gripped my arm. "Hey, hold on. You heard Miss Austin."

I jerked back. "Let go!" I yelled. "I need to see if she's okay."

But he didn't let go. He pulled me up tight against him. "I know you want to be with her. But you'll be in the doctors' way if you go barging in there. Let them do their job."

My heartbeat thrashed in my ears, and it was hard to breathe. I pressed my face against Trey's chest and started to bawl. "She's supposed to be getting better."

"I know, Tiger."

I'd never been held that tightly before, so hard it hurt my ribs. But there was something that felt safe about it, too, and after a little bit I quit feeling so out of control.

"You okay now?" Trey asked.

"Yeah," I whimpered, even though I'd never felt less okay in my life. He relaxed his grip and walked me across the room to the vinyl couch where Marti sat. I collapsed beside her, and she pulled me against her shoulder. "It's gonna be okay, Poppy. Try to be brave."

"I don't wanna be brave," I cried. "I just want things to be like they used to be."

Miss Austin brought me over a tissue. Then she perched on the edge of one of the lime-colored chairs across the room. Trey stayed standing near the door. Nobody spoke for a long time. The coffeepot in the corner gurgled and hissed. A call for a Dr. Burris crackled over the intercom.

Miss Austin opened her purse, took out her cell phone, and began texting. Every few minutes it gently vibrated with a reply. Finally she puffed out a breath and gave Marti an anxious look. "Will you be able to stay here with Poppy for a while longer? I'm afraid I have some things that can't wait."

"Of course," Marti said. "I'll stay as long as it takes."

"Thank you, I really appreciate it." She stepped over to me. "I'm so sorry about your grandma, Poppy. I promise to check in soon, okay?"

I looked up at her but didn't answer. She had on those stupid dangling earrings again. She flitted with her hair and then tapped her way out of the room. I could tell when she reached the elevator because the tapping stopped. "She always has stuff that can't wait," I mumbled.

Marti patted my hair. "She does have a full plate, Poppy."

Trey stepped out into the hall to take a phone call. When he came back a few minutes later, a gray-haired doctor followed. "Are any of you here for Bethany Parker?"

I sat up. "She's my grandma."

"I'm Dr. Corliss," he said, looking between the three of us. "We've got her stabilized for now. Her vital signs are good, but her oxygen level is very low. It'll be at least twenty-four hours before we're able to ascertain the amount of damage. Nobody at the nursing home seems to know exactly when she had the stroke."

"What made her have another one?" I asked.

Dr. Corliss gave me a kind look, like he felt bad he had to answer a question like that. "Your grandma's had a series of mild mini-strokes, and unfortunately, they often lead to bigger, more serious ones."

I swallowed. "Can I see her?"

He nodded. "You can go in for a minute. But I'm afraid she won't know you're there."

"I don't care. I want to anyway."

Marti stood. "I'll go with you."

The doctor started out of the room but then turned back. "Do any of you know if Mrs. Parker has a durable power of attorney?"

"I'll check on it," Trey said.

Grandma Beth lay in a mostly white room, underneath all-white bedding. She had a tube in her arm and an oxygen mask over half her face. A dark green bottle was attached to a machine that made sharp hushing noises every few seconds.

It made me sick to see her looking so helpless. I reached out and touched her hand. "She's cold."

Marti pulled the blanket higher on Grandma Beth's chest. "I doubt she feels cold, honey. It's probably just her hands."

I wrapped my fingers around Grandma Beth's wrist. Her pulse throbbed as soft as a feather's touch — so softly I barely felt it. I wanted to tell her I loved her, that everything would be okay, and to just sleep as long as she needed. But it felt like somebody had me by the throat. And the worst part was that the doctor was right — Grandma Beth *didn't* know I was there. It almost felt like she wasn't there herself.

Later, I spent most of that afternoon lying on Marti's couch pretending to watch a movie. But my mind was numb with guilt over lying to Trey and worry over Grandma Beth, and I knew if I didn't find some way to let the pressure out, I'd go crazy. There was no way I could explain what I'd done to Marti or Trey or even Grandma Beth, if she'd been awake. They wouldn't understand, and who could blame them? But then it finally came to me — there was one person who might understand. Someone who'd made her own stupid mistakes. I pulled out my cell phone to text Lizzie.

Hi. What R U doing?

My phone buzzed with a reply only seconds later.

Hi. Cleaning dog kennels.

I sucked in a breath. Lizzie was at the shelter. I found Marti in the kitchen, rolling out pizza dough, her hands covered in flour. "Hey there," she said. "Like pizza?"

I nodded.

"Great. It's one of the few things I ever make from scratch. Want to help?"

"Actually, I was wondering if we could go to the shelter for a while."

"It's closed today, honey. It's Sunday."

"I know. But Lizzie and Carol are there. Besides, I really want to visit Gunner."

The rolling pin stopped, and Marti's eyes clouded with worry. "Gunner's beautiful, Poppy. But he's . . . he's got an uncertain future. Don't get attached to him."

I let out a soft breath. *An uncertain future.* Those words made me want to start bawling again, because she wasn't just describing Gunner — she was describing me. I turned my palms up. "I know," I said. "I just really need to see him. Just for a few minutes. Please?"

Marti sealed her lips. I watched as she patted the dough into a circle and waited for her to say no. But instead she nodded. "All right, as soon as I get the dough ready to rise."

Carol's car was the only one in the shelter parking lot. Marti went inside, and I slipped around back to Gunner's kennel. He stood and stared intently as soon as he caught sight of me. "Hey there, boy. How are you doin', Gunner? What a good dog."

The low growl came at about ten feet again, but this time I didn't let it bother me. I kept moving forward, ever so slowly, and Gunner continued to growl. But he finally stopped once I knelt down on the scrubby grass right outside his kennel and started to talk to him.

After about ten minutes, he quit acting nervous and sat to observe me from a few feet away. I kept talking, telling him how handsome he was and how he could be a dog movie star if he wanted. After a while, his ears pricked up and he looked past me.

I turned, expecting it to be Marti. But it was Lizzie. "Figured you'd be out here," she said.

"Hey," I said.

She gestured toward Gunner. "Usually he has a fit if anybody gets too close."

"He's not mean. You just have to be quiet and move slow. Give him time to get used to you." I patted the ground beside me. "You can come sit if you want."

Lizzie hesitated a few seconds more before she moved closer and gingerly sat down on the grass. Gunner watched her every move, but he didn't growl.

"See," I said. "He's okay."

Lizzie started pulling up blades of grass and making a little pile beside her leg. "Marti says your grandma's not doing so great."

I swallowed. "No. She had another stroke."

"That stinks."

"Yeah," I said, and my heart started to pound like when I'd seen the poster of William Eugene Frank. "Lizzie, can I ask you something . . . kinda personal?"

A guarded look came over her face, like she was afraid it was some kind of trap. "Maybe."

"That day you spray-painted the federal building, what made you do it?"

She didn't answer for a minute, but her throat bobbed as she swallowed. She leaned back on her arms. "I dunno. I was just so . . . mad."

"Mad at who?"

"At my parents. For all the stupid arguing, and for getting divorced, and for never asking me how I felt about any of it."

That caught me up short. I had no idea Carol was divorced. "Sorry. I didn't know. When did it happen?"

"Last year."

"That must have been really tough."

She released a slow, even breath. "People get divorced all the time, but you never see it happening to your parents, you know? I mean, one day everything seems okay, everything's like you're used to. And then the next thing, your parents drop this bomb on you. We're splitting up. Decision made. Live with it." She rolled her eyes. "They have no idea what it feels like, what it does to you."

I nodded and tried to think of something to say, to tell her it all made sense.

"It's not like I thought getting in trouble would actually fix anything," she said. "I just felt like I was gonna explode I was so mad. I actually wanted to get in trouble, to cause them trouble, you know? To make them pay somehow." Her breath hitched on that last word and she looked down, embarrassed. "Sounds pretty lame, huh?"

I sniffed and shook my head. I wanted to tell her how many times I'd felt that same exact anger myself. Anger at my parents for leaving me with Grandma Beth, for not loving me enough to stay home. But Lizzie didn't know that part of my story. "No," I said softly, "it actually makes perfect sense."

A slight motion caught my eye as Gunner turned in a

circle and then calmly lay down, like he was settling in for what he knew might be a long conversation.

"So," I said, "if you could go back, would you do it again?"

Lizzie smirked. "No way. It's practically wrecked my life." She gave me a close look. "Why'd you want to know all this anyway?"

Why? It was another of those simple questions I had no idea how to answer. All I knew was that my guilt was about to suffocate me if I didn't let it out. And even though crying in front of Lizzie was the last thing I wanted to do, the emotion came flooding up anyway.

"Because," I whispered, "I think I just wrecked my life, too."

She drew back a little, like she thought I might be contagious or something. "Oh," she said. Then she took a quick look over her shoulder and lowered her voice. "So . . . are you gonna tell me?"

I knew I was taking a chance, because I didn't even know Lizzie that well. But I started to talk anyway, and everything gushed out like I'd turned on both faucets full blast, and I couldn't have stopped if I'd wanted to. I told her about Grandma Beth's second stroke, about how sick she really was, and about how scared I was. I told her more about Lindsay getting shot and about William Eugene Frank, and then I told her how I'd lied to Trey.

134

And Lizzie kept her mouth shut and listened, with her eyebrows arched a little, like she couldn't quite believe such an interesting story could come from somebody like me.

"Whoa," she said when I finished. "You did get yourself in deep poop." Then she smiled. "Thought you said your life was only G-rated."

And I smiled, too, because it was a pretty funny comment even though I didn't feel like laughing. "I told you it used to be G. But it's more like PG-13 now, remember?"

"No kidding." She squinted at me. "But you don't really believe you made your grandma have another stroke, though, right? 'Cause that's not how stuff happens."

I sniffled. "I don't know what I believe anymore." I looked over at Gunner and made eye contact with him. "Hey, boy," I said. "Now you know my secret, too."

"So what are you gonna do?" Lizzie asked. "About that Frank guy?"

"I don't know. What *can* I do?"

"But don't you want the cops to catch him? I mean, aren't you scared he might be looking for you?"

I swallowed. "Maybe a little. I don't know. I think I'm more scared that Grandma Beth won't get better, and I'll have to spend the rest of my life at the center."

"So what's it like at that place?"

I rolled my eyes. "It's awful. Everything about it stinks. It's crowded, there's not enough hot water, and the food's no good. But mainly, it's not home. I hate it."

Lizzie was quiet for a minute, then she let out a soft sigh. "I'm supposed to spend every other weekend with Dad."

The change of subject sent me spinning for a few seconds. "Then why don't you?"

"Because it's like what you just said, it's not home. He's got an apartment now, and his girlfriend, Kimberly, and her kid, Jake, are always over there, and it just feels so weird."

"Is Kimberly nice to you?"

Lizzie tipped her head to the side. "She tries to be. I mean, she asks me what I like to eat and how school's going and stuff like that, like she's trying to be all friendly."

"Is that a bad thing?"

"Yeah. Because, I mean, I have a mom. And I don't wanna be her friend. So I don't know how to act around her."

"What's Jake like?"

She shrugged. "He's eight, and he's kind of a pain. He always wants me to play computer games with him."

"Is his dad around?"

"I'm not sure. I think he took off when he was little."

I cringed inside. "He's probably lonely."

Lizzie looked at me. "Why?"

"Well, if he's the only kid, and he doesn't have his own dad, then he's probably . . . lonely."

She studied me with a curious look, and I was worried I'd said too much. But then Lizzie nodded, like maybe that hadn't occurred to her. "You never told me why you live at the kids' center."

It took me a second to realize she'd changed the subject again, and my muscles tensed at her question. "You know why. Because my grandma had a stroke."

"Yeah, but why do you live with her? What happened to your parents?"

I glanced at Gunner. He lay quietly, with his head resting on his paws. I felt my heart squeeze at the thought of having to explain about my parents to another person. "I can't right now," I said. "Maybe another time."

She shrugged, but I could tell she was disappointed. "Yeah, okay."

Without thinking, I stuck my fingertip through the wire into Gunner's kennel and wiggled it at him.

Lizzie drew in a breath. "Better watch it."

Gunner studied my finger for a few seconds, then he stood and cautiously stepped forward and brushed it with his nose. "Good boy," I whispered. "What a good dog, Gunner."

And then I stuck all my fingers through, and he moved a step closer, like he'd just been waiting for somebody to try and be his friend. And I touched his long whiskers and the thick, coarse hair on his neck, and it felt like I'd won a prize.

Lizzie whistled softly in admiration. "Guess he likes you."

"Yeah, well we're both kind of like prisoners, so we can relate to each other."

She grinned. "Makes sense to me."

I pulled my hand away from Gunner and checked my cell phone. Forty-five minutes had passed. "I should go. Marti's probably waiting for me. Promise you won't tell anybody what we talked about."

"I won't if you won't."

I reluctantly stood. "Thanks for . . . you know, letting me spill to you."

She smiled. "Sure. But remember, only the first session's free. After this, there's a hundred-dollar spill fee."

Trey wasn't there for supper that night, and I was so glad, since he was the last person I wanted to see. After I finished my pizza, I called the hospital to check on Grandma Beth. She was the same, the nurse told me, but resting comfortably. She promised to call if anything changed overnight.

Marti offered me some chamomile bath soap and sent me to take a bubble bath. By the time I finished soaking in the hot water, I was nearly asleep. I got into my pajamas, gave Marti a hug good night, and fell into bed. But as soon as I tucked my hand under the pillow, a sharp crinkling sound made me jump back up and flip on the light. And I stood there, staring, as all the guilt I'd managed to push aside came roaring back.

Right beside my pillow lay the Twinkie Trey told me I'd earned — two, in fact — my reward for lying to the police.

There was no change in Grandma Beth over the next two days, but on the third day she finally woke up. Trey took me to see her. She'd been moved from the intensive-care unit to a regular room. A thin purple curtain hid her bed from view as we walked in, but I heard the familiar hushing sound coming from the oxygen machine. I hesitated in front of the curtain, afraid of what I might find when I pulled it back.

Trey gave me a nudge. "Go ahead, you check on her first."

I moved the curtain aside a few inches and peeked around. Three bright red poppies stood in a glass vase on the windowsill, looking like they owned the room. "Grandma Beth," I said. "It's me, Poppy. Are you awake?"

She turned her head toward me. An oxygen mask covered her mouth and nose, but I could tell she was smiling from the way her eyes crinkled at the corners. She reached up and lowered the mask. "Oh, Poppy."

The sound of her voice paralyzed me for a few seconds. Her words sounded slow and strange, almost like her tongue was too thick. I moved up beside her, leaned down, and kissed her on the cheek. "I was so scared for you," I whispered. "Are you feeling okay now?"

"I'm okay."

"Does it hurt to talk?"

She gently moved her head to the side. "Just harder."

"Does the oxygen help?"

Her eyes flickered with confusion. "Oxygen?"

My heart sank. I pointed toward the oxygen machine. "Yeah, you know, the oxygen coming from the mask. Does it help?"

"Oh," she said. "Yes." She moved the mask back into place and took a couple of deep, slow breaths before pulling it down again. "Who's with you?"

"Trey."

"Have him come in."

Trey pushed aside the curtain and stepped in. "Mrs. Parker," he said. "It's sure good to see you again."

Grandma Beth didn't smile. She looked him up and down for a long moment, and I wondered what she was thinking. Then she gathered a breath and said, "Thank you for looking after my girl."

"You're welcome. She's a great kid."

His words made me cringe inside. If he only knew.

Grandma Beth looked at me. "That she is." She held the mask back in place for several seconds.

"Who brought you the flowers?" I asked.

Grandma Beth slowly turned her head toward the windowsill. She studied the poppies for several seconds with her lips pressed together, before looking back to me. "I forgot."

I stepped over to the flowers, but there was no card.

"Marti," Grandma Beth suddenly said, sounding pleased with herself.

I gaped in surprise. "You got to meet Marti? She's Trey's mom."

"Yes. Very sweet."

I wondered when she'd had time to stop by, but before I could ask, Grandma Beth said, "Poppy, I need coffee."

"Are you supposed to have coffee?"

She smiled. "Don't tell the nurses."

I gave her a close look. "Are you trying to get rid of me?"

"Never."

"Then why are you making me leave when I just got here?"

"Priscilla Marie," she said with obvious effort, "coffee, please."

I reluctantly nodded. "Okay," I said. I frowned at Trey, and he moved out of my way with a smile.

There was no coffee in the nearest waiting area, of course. I had to take the elevator two floors down to the maternity ward before I found a pot. But then there were no sugar packets, only cream. I finally tracked down some sugar. If Grandma's plan was to send me on a wild-goose chase, it had worked like a charm.

By the time I rounded the corner back to her room, Trey was just coming out. "Your turn," he said. "I'll be back up in a bit."

Grandma had raised the bed so she was more on my level. It wasn't until I held the coffee cup out to her that I realized she couldn't lift her right arm.

I held it to her lips and tipped it ever so slowly, so it wouldn't burn her, but a trickle of coffee still dribbled down her chin. "It's okay," she said.

So we tried again, and it worked better the second time. "Mmm. Thank you."

I sat down in the chair next to her and waited while she breathed in more oxygen. I hated seeing her struggle to talk. It made me feel so helpless. "Did the doctor say how long you have to stay here this time?"

She cleared her throat. "No. But we have to let our . . . our . . ."

"Our what, Grandma?"

She stared up at the ceiling with a baffled look, and I could see her struggling to come up with the correct word. "Our . . . house?" she asked uncertainly.

"Our apartment?"

"Yes. We have to . . . let it go."

I stared at her, sure she must still be confused. "Let it go? What do you mean?"

"Can't keep paying . . . if we're not there."

I felt like somebody had whacked me from behind. "But what about when you get out? Where will we live?"

She put the mask back in place and took several more breaths. "They'll send me back to . . . to the care home."

"The Huckleberry Home?" I wanted to be strong, but I couldn't be. The panic rose up into my chest, and I started to cry. "But if you don't come home, what will happen to me? I don't want to live at the center. I hate it there."

"Oh, Poppy," she said. "I'm so sorry. I've let you down." And her eyes filled with tears, too, and I couldn't stand to see it.

"No," I said. "No, you haven't." And I dropped my head down on her blankets.

She smoothed my hair. "There, there," she said in her thick, halting voice. "Change is hard, remember?"

And I nodded, because I knew exactly what she was talking about. It was one of her favorite quotes. *"All changes, even the most longed for, have their melancholy; for what we leave behind us is a part of ourselves; we must die to one life before we can enter another."*

I even knew the author — a man named Anatole France. But right then, I couldn't bear to think about him or his quote, because I hated them both.

Chapter Ten

BY THE time Trey and I walked out of the hospital, my legs were shaky and I felt like I weighed a thousand pounds. I crawled into the front seat of the car, glad to be off my feet.

Trey's leather jacket made squeaking noises as he settled into the driver's seat. He stuck the key in the ignition but didn't start the engine. I stared out the windshield at a lady walking her Chihuahua across the grassy strip between the street and the parking lot. The little dog pranced along, its head held high, like it belonged in some royal court. "I thought she was gonna get better," I said.

"She still might, Tiger."

"What's that *durable power of attorney* thing the doctor asked if Grandma had the other day?"

"A medical directive. It lets you make decisions about your health care ahead of time."

"Ahead of what?"

"Before an emergency comes up."

"What kind of decisions?"

"About what treatment you'll accept, whether or not you'll take a blood transfusion. Whether or not you want to be resuscitated if your heart stops . . . that sort of thing."

"What's *resuscitated*?"

"That's when the doctor tries to get your heart beating again."

I didn't understand. "But if he didn't, you'd die. Who wouldn't want to be resuscitated?"

He tipped his head. "Death isn't always a bad thing, Poppy."

That gave me a start. How could death ever be a *good* thing, unless maybe you were in severe pain or something. It didn't make sense. But I didn't have the energy for such a complicated subject right then.

Trey reached over and gave my knee a squeeze. Then he started the car.

The lady and her Chihuahua crossed the street in front of us and started up the other side. The little dog was all business now, trotting fast, straining at the leash. My hip started to tingle, and it took me a minute to realize it was my cell phone. It was a text from Lizzie.

146

Gunner needs U. Hurry.

The message gave me a dropping sensation in my stomach. My thumbs flew over the keyboard. *What's wrong?*

Just hurry.

A shudder passed through me, and I looked at Trey.

He raised his eyebrows.

"Could we stop by the animal shelter real quick? Just for a few minutes?"

"What's going on?"

I hesitated. He didn't like Lizzie. Would he take me if he knew the message was from her? "I was just wondering if you might want to meet a good friend of mine. He's pretty cool."

"At the shelter?"

"It won't take long. He's not much of a talker."

Trey cracked a smile. "He must have four legs."

Relief flowed through me. "Yeah, actually he does."

He shifted the gear. "Okay, but then I have to get back to work."

A few minutes later we pulled into the shelter's parking lot. There were only four vehicles — Carol's car, a pickup with SAND CREEK VETERINARY painted along the side, and two others.

I wanted to find Lizzie, but something told me to go

straight back and check on Gunner. I gestured for Trey to follow me along the far side of the building. "Come on," I said, "he's out back in his own kennel."

Trey glanced around. "Maybe you better check in with Carol first."

"No, it's okay. She won't mind."

"Why isn't he with the other dogs?"

"Uh . . . I'm not sure," I said, because I couldn't think of anything better.

I caught a glimpse of Gunner resting with his head on his paws, but then he rose with one smooth move, his whole body rigid. He was so beautiful. I wondered why Lizzie had sent the text. Everything seemed fine.

"Hey there," I said. "Take it easy, boy, it's just me."

His ears flickered, and he gave a single sweep of his tail. It was the first time I'd seen him do that. I looked up at Trey. "His name's Gunner. Isn't he pretty?"

"So this is the good friend, huh?"

"Yeah, but he's kind of shy with new people, so you should probably stay out here." Then, without giving myself time to chicken out, I unlatched the kennel gate and stepped inside. Gunner took a step back. I knelt beside him and slowly reached an arm around his neck. "Good boy," I said. "You are such a good dog. Yes, you are."

He touched my face with his nose and sniffed at my shirt.

"He must be up for adoption?"

I felt a little jab to my heart. "Yeah, I wish I could have him. But he needs a place with a big yard and no little kids . . . at least no little boys. He likes to bite boys."

Trey smirked. "Did he tell you that?"

"No, the guy who brought him in."

"Oh. Maybe you shouldn't be in there."

"It's okay. He's fine around me."

"Has he been here long?"

"A few weeks."

"He probably needs a job," Trey said. "Shepherds like to work."

Gunner's ears flicked back and forth as Trey spoke, but he'd relaxed enough to lean into me like I was leaning into him. And as I ran my fingers through his warm, thick fur, I felt myself start to relax a little, too.

But after only a few minutes, the sound of Carol's voice snapped me to attention. She was talking to another woman, someone whose voice I didn't recognize, and they were coming in our direction.

I started to stand, because my first thought was to get out of the kennel before Carol saw me. But then I realized that maybe this was as good a chance as any to let her see Gunner and me together, to prove that he was perfectly safe, and not aggressive at all.

I slipped a finger under his collar and settled back into him. "Take it easy, boy. It's just Carol. You know her."

Trey narrowed his eyes, like he sensed something was up. Then he stepped away from the kennel and waved a hand. "Hey, Carol."

There was a pause, followed by her squeal of surprise. "Trey! Well, hello there, stranger. How have you been?"

"Oh, can't complain. How about you? Mom tells me you're living on the South Hill now."

I took a deep breath and tightened my hold on Gunner. "Hang on," I whispered. "This might turn out to be a good thing."

"Were you looking for your mom?" Carol asked. "Because I don't expect her until tomorrow."

"No, Mom's home. Poppy just talked me into stopping by."

"Poppy?" Carol's voice rose into a high-pitched question mark. "She's here?"

"Well, yeah . . . she said you wouldn't mind."

Carol hurried into view and skidded to a stop next to Trey.

I forced a smile. "Hey, Carol."

Our eyes met, and she froze. "Poppy! What in the world . . . You know you're not allowed to be in there."

"She's not?" Trey said.

I knew it was one of the worst times ever to laugh, but I couldn't help it. There was just something genuinely funny about seeing adults look at each other all confused like that. "It's okay," I said quickly, "Gunner's great, Carol. Just look at him. He's being really good."

Carol seemed to come unfrozen then and her nostrils flared, and it was pretty obvious she didn't find anything funny about the situation. "Yes, I see that," she said. "Now come out of there anyway."

"But why? Gunner's fine. He'd never hurt me."

Trey coughed. "Man, I'm sorry, Carol. I asked her if she needed to check in or anything."

Carol touched her fingertips to her forehead. "No, no, it's not your fault. It's just that Gunner's got a history of aggression. I can't trust him — that's why he's out here instead of with the other dogs."

I lowered my eyes and focused on massaging Gunner's neck.

"So, this must be Gunner?" the other lady asked, her voice hesitant. She was tall and thin, and carried a small black bag.

Carol nodded, and her shoulders slumped. "Yes, this is Gunner, and you'll have to excuse my poor manners. Trey and Poppy, I'd like you to meet Dr. Julie Buchard, from Sand Creek Veterinary."

"Hi," I said.

Trey stuck out his hand. "Trey Brannigan, ma'am. Nice to meet you."

The lady smiled. "Oh, call me Dr. Julie, please. *Ma'am* makes me feel way too old." Silence followed the introductions. Trey shoved his hands into his back pockets. Carol and Dr. Julie kept glancing around — at me, at each other, at the ground — acting like two nervous little kids.

That's when I caught a glimpse of Lizzie, standing near the corner of the building where no one else could see her. She flattened her hand and drew it across her throat in a quick gesture. And right then is when everything finally made sense.

Lizzie's text — Dr. Julie — the black bag — Carol's shock at seeing me.

I'd thought she was just surprised to see me inside Gunner's kennel. But she wasn't. She was surprised to see me *at all*. I wasn't supposed to be there. I'd interrupted something.

Tears instantly flooded my eyes, and I glared at Carol. "I'm not coming out, and you're not touching him. He's a good dog. He didn't do anything wrong."

Trey did a double take.

Carol looked up at the sky. "You know," she said, to no one in particular, "some days this job really sucks."

Dr. Julie cleared her throat. "It's fine. You can call me if you need to . . . reschedule."

"No," I yelled, "you're not rescheduling."

Gunner pulled away and started twirling in nervous circles.

Carol turned pale and made a low shushing sound with her voice. "Okay, okay now, let's all be calm. The last thing we want is for Gunner to get worked up." She stepped over to the kennel door and eased it open. She held a hand out toward me. "Honey, I understand why you're upset, but you're upsetting Gunner, too, and I'm not sure what he might do if he feels threatened. You need to please come out now and give him a chance to calm down."

I rubbed a hand across my eyes and tried to steady my voice. "I'm *not* coming out, Carol. Not unless you promise that you won't do anything to him."

She bit her bottom lip, and a mask of sadness covered

her face. "You know," she said softly, "the last animal I had Dr. Julie put down was a fifteen-year-old cat with stomach cancer. I'd only known him for two days, and I still cried over it. So don't think I don't understand how you're feeling, okay? And I promise you, Poppy, if you come out, Gunner will still be here tomorrow when you and Marti come. Okay?"

I took a shaky breath. "You really promise?"

"Scout's honor. Now hold up your end of the bargain and come out of there."

I looked at Gunner. He stared back with his deep chocolate eyes, almost like he was assuring me that everything would be okay. I stood on weak knees and crept out of the kennel. I looked over toward Lizzie, but she was gone.

Carol latched the gate behind me and blew out a breath. "Well, now! I'm glad that's over with. You know, Poppy, if all my volunteers were as volatile as you, I'm not sure I could cope."

I wasn't sure what the word *volatile* meant, but Dr. Julie smiled.

Carol put her arm around me and gave me a quick squeeze before she turned me toward Trey. "Okay, Detective Brannigan, she's all yours. Handcuffs are optional."

As soon as I got back to Marti's, I looked up the word *volatile*. It meant *unpredictable, hot-blooded, impulsive*. And for some crazy reason that definition made me grin, especially the impulsive part, because that's what Grandma Beth called me, too. And it was almost a comfort to know that even if everything else was changing, at least my reputation was still the same.

By the time Marti and I reached the shelter the next morning, I couldn't wait to see Gunner. Because even though Marti had assured me that Carol wouldn't go back on a promise, and Lizzie had texted to tell me he was fine, I couldn't rest until I saw for myself. But there he was, sitting at his kennel gate, waiting for me.

"Hey, boy! Hi, Gunner." I knew I probably wasn't supposed to go in with him, but I didn't care. I opened his kennel and threw my arms around his neck. "Man, it's good to see you. Wanna go for a walk? Maybe now that Carol knows you're not vicious, she'll let me take you out. Huh, what do you think about that?" I kept talking to him for another few minutes, until I sensed someone behind me. I turned to find Lizzie watching.

"You're brave," she said.

I grinned at her as a wave of appreciation washed over me. "Thanks for yesterday. You saved him, you know?"

She shook her head. "Not really. You did that."

"Yeah, but if you hadn't sent that text . . ." I paused as an awful shudder passed through me. "Yesterday was really rough already. I don't think I could've handled it if something happened to Gunner."

"Did something more happen with your grandma?"

"She's just not doing good. It's really hard for her to talk now. Her voice is all funny and weird, and sometimes she can't think of the word she wants."

"Sorry."

"Yeah." I took a deep breath to calm myself. "So, did your mom say anything more about what happened with Gunner?"

"No. I don't think she knows I had anything to do with it."

"Well, you did really good. Especially for somebody who doesn't like dogs."

She shrugged. "It's not like I hate them. They just never seem to like me."

I looked at Gunner and ran my fingertips over his muzzle. "They're not like people. You don't have to bend over backward to please them. All you have to do is give them a little attention, and they'll love you forever."

Lizzie smirked and gave me a goofy smile. "You're starting to sound like a commercial."

"Well, it's true," I said. "That's why I like dogs better than I like most people."

"Let me guess: You probably want to be a vet someday?"

I shook my head. "No. Vets have to do too many sad things. But I'd like to do something with animals. I'd really like to illustrate kids' picture books. What do you want to do when you grow up?"

"I'm gonna be a cosmetologist."

I massaged Gunner's neck and tried to remember exactly what that word meant. "That's to do with cutting hair, right?"

"Yeah, but it's also stuff like makeup and facials."

I remembered what Marti had said about her pink highlights and had to bite my tongue to keep from telling Lizzie. "Did you do your own highlights?"

"Yeah."

"That's cool," I said, "because they look totally professional."

Lizzie seemed to stand a little straighter all of a sudden,

and it made me feel so good for saying it. "Thanks," she said. "I could do yours sometime if you want."

I grinned. "I dunno what my grandma would say about pink hair."

"It wouldn't have to be pink. We could just do some sun streaks or something. They look really good on brown hair like yours."

"Yeah," I said. "That might be fun." I gave Gunner another pat and stood up. "I'm gonna go ask your mom if I can take him out on a walk. Think she'll let me?"

Lizzie shrugged and backed up as I eased out of the kennel. "Maybe. She's probably in her office."

"Okay, I'll go see." I hurried through the back door of the shelter, headed for Carol's office, and nearly ran right into her. She was talking with a police officer. I came up short. "Woops, sorry."

Carol wiggled her eyebrows at me. "Well, hello there, Poppy. Greg, this is one of my volunteer dog walkers. Poppy, this is Officer Greg Kinsley. He's with the K-9 unit."

I took a closer look at him. "Oh, I remember you," I blurted. "You're Dozer's handler."

His bushy eyebrows jumped. "Have we met?"

I shook my head and gave him a brief rundown of the night at the gas station. "Aha," he said, "good memory."

Carol smiled. "Anyway, Greg, I'll be glad to keep my eye out for you, but I thought the department was buying from European breeders."

"For the patrol dogs we do. The criteria isn't so rigid for narcotics. But they need to be under three years old, without a history of behavioral issues."

Carol snorted. "No issues? Shoot, we all have issues."

"I know. I just thought I'd check since we've had decent luck with shelter dogs before."

I looked back and forth between them, trying to make sense of the conversation. "You can use shelter dogs for police work?"

"Sometimes."

Carol nodded. "Two of our puppies went to the Border Patrol last year. And we've had several chosen for training as service dogs."

"You mean like for people with disabilities?"

"Yep." She looked back at Officer Kinsley. "At any rate, you know our turnover rate is pretty constant, so I'll give you a call if I find one who fits the bill."

My heart started to pound. Narcotics? He was looking for a drug-sniffing dog? Why didn't she tell him about Gunner?

"Good enough," he said. He tipped his head. "Ladies."

"Wait," I said. "I know a dog that might work."

Carol's eyes sparked with surprise. "You do?" she said, and then just as fast her smile faded, and she smacked her forehead. "Oh, no, Poppy."

"What?" I said. "He's young and super smart and really pretty."

"Yeeeeees, he is. He's also totally unsuitable for the position in question."

Officer Kinsley looked like he wanted to laugh. "I'm sensing a little dissention here."

Carol looked toward the sky without tilting her head. "Poppy has taken a real liking to one of our dogs. He's handsome as all get-out, but he's got a history."

"What sort of history?"

"People claim he bites," I said, "but he's real friendly to me. You just have to let him warm up to you."

"It's not just a claim, Poppy. He bit a young boy; that's why he's here, remember?"

"That's what the guy told you, but nobody knows the real story. Remember?" I added.

Carol's lips parted, but no sound came out.

"How old is he?" Officer Kinsley asked.

"Young," I said. "Probably eighteen months or so. Right, Carol?"

"Does he know any of the basics? Sit, stay, come?"

"I'm not sure yet," I said. "But I can teach him whatever he needs to know. Do you want to see him?"

Carol sighed. I knew she was about to say no way, but something in my face must have stopped her. "When did you say the program starts, Greg?"

"Four weeks."

"That's hardly any time at all, Poppy."

"It's plenty of time," I said. "He'll learn fast. I know he will."

I held my breath as Carol stared at me, and I could tell she was trying to figure out just what to do with such an unpredictable, hot-blooded, impulsive kid. But then she broke into a grin and threw her hands up. "I still say he's totally unsuitable, Greg. But Poppy won't be happy until you at least look at him."

He winked at me. "Lead the way."

I was so surprised that it took a second for his words to register. "Really? Okay. He's out this way." I wasn't a very experienced prayer, but I prayed the whole thirty seconds it took to reach Gunner's kennel.

"Hey, boy," I called softly, giving him as much forewarning as I could. "Hey there, Gunner."

He rose in the same impressive way he always did — in a single smooth motion — but his eyes focused on the stranger at my side.

Officer Kinsley gave a low whistle. "Hey there, big guy. You are one good-looking dog. You look like a dog I had when I was a kid. Yes, you do."

Gunner flicked an ear back and forth, listening to the new voice. Then, after a minute, Officer Kinsley pulled a key chain from his front pocket and jangled it. Then he dragged his knuckles across the kennel several times, and it made a harsh drumming sound. I didn't know what he was trying to do, and I could tell Gunner didn't, either. He gave a low growl.

My heart sank. "Gunner," I scolded.

"No, it's okay" he said. "A little aggression can be a good thing. Plus he's not so much aggressive as he is wary."

"He is?"

"Sure. Look at his posture. A dog's body language speaks volumes. His is more, 'I'm keeping a close eye on you,' rather than, 'I want to tear you to pieces.' See how he carries himself?"

I welled up with pride. "He's beautiful, isn't he?"

Officer Kinsley stood there a few more minutes, watching Gunner and sharing tidbits of dog-training wisdom with me. Then he said, "Tell you what, no promises, but if you can teach him sit, stay, and come in the next three weeks, I'll come back and see how he handles for me on a leash. Think you can do it?"

I had to fight hard to keep from throwing my arms around him. "I know I can."

I gave Carol a glance of triumph, and she shook her head as we walked Officer Kinsley back to his patrol car. As soon as he pulled away, she turned to me with her hands on her hips. "Okay, Poppy Parker. You want to explain to me what just happened here?"

I raised my hands in surrender, but I couldn't keep the grin off my face. "Nothing. Just trying to give a great dog a chance. That's what the shelter's all about, right?"

"Was yesterday the first time you've been inside Gunner's kennel?"

"Yeah. But I petted him through the wire before that and he's always been fine."

She groaned. "You could've been badly bitten."

"He won't bite me," I said. "I keep telling you, that kid he did bite probably deserved it."

Carol seemed to think about things for a minute, and then she puffed out her cheeks. "All right, you listen to me. In light of what you just committed to, you may work with

Gunner, but not alone. I want somebody else with you just in case. And you can only work with him in the enclosure with no other dogs in there. Understood?"

I straightened and gave her a salute. "Yes, ma'am."

She laughed as she wagged a finger at me. "Don't you give me attitude. I have to put up with enough of that from Eliza May."

"Can I ask her to help me?"

"Sure. If you can talk her into it."

"Can I start working with him now?"

She snorted and turned on her heel. "Seeing as how you have less than a month, I suggest you do."

I found Lizzie in the Kitty Palace wearing rubber gloves and carrying a bottle of bleach. "Hey," I said, "want a much better job?"

"Such as?"

"Working with Gunner."

She gave me a startled look. "Mom's gonna let you?"

"Yeah, but it's even better than that. If I can teach him all the basics, he might get considered to be a police dog."

"No way."

I couldn't keep the grin off my face as I gave her the short version of what had just happened with Officer Kinsley. "But I can't work with him alone," I said. "I need somebody out there in case Gunner decides to rip me to shreds. You can sit under the tree and play Angry Birds if you want."

"I would," Lizzie said. "But my stupid phone's dead. I forgot to charge it last night."

"Then you can use mine."

Her eyes lit up, and she put a finger to her lips. "Okay, then, but don't tell Mom. I'm supposed to be working."

I hunted up a leather lead and a tennis ball, and went back out to Gunner's kennel. He wagged his tail when he saw it was just me. I opened his kennel door and took his muzzle in both hands. "We're gonna do this. You and me, boy. You're gonna become a narcotics dog and help catch bad guys. You wanna do that, Gunner? I am, you know? I'm helping to catch . . ."

But my own words brought me up short and made my face tingle. Who was I trying to fool? I wasn't helping to catch a bad guy; I was helping to keep one out on the street. I shook my head as the sickening reality surged through me. How could I have made a decision like that? When had I gotten so selfish?

Gunner's eyes bored into me like he could read my thoughts. "Okay," I whispered. "I'll fix it. I'll talk to Trey. I'll do it tonight, promise."

Lizzie ambled over a few minutes later, and I handed her my phone before I led Gunner out. She backed off a few steps. "You're sure he won't bite me?"

I bent down and looked into Gunner's eyes. "See this girl right here? She saved your life yesterday, so I don't wanna hear so much as a snarl directed her way, ever, got it?"

Lizzie laughed. "Wow, thanks. I feel so much better now." She retreated under the big oak tree while I took Gunner into the enclosure. It took me less than a minute to learn two things about him. He already knew how to sit, and he couldn't have cared less about playing with a tennis ball. We jogged several laps to burn off energy, and then I placed him in a sit and put my hand up. "Stay," I commanded, and backed off two steps. "Stay."

He let me get about five feet away before he bounded toward me. I put him back in a sit and tried again. But each time he did the same thing. After about ten failed attempts I started to get a little scared. When I was nine years old, I'd taught my Lab, Lucy, to sit and to shake hands — that was about the limit of my dog-training experience. What if I couldn't do it? What if Gunner couldn't learn? But then I looked into his dark eyes, and I knew he could. "Okay, come on," I said, "let's just walk some more."

"Hey," Lizzie called, "you've got pictures of the cactus house at Manito Park."

I glanced over, surprised. My first thought was to ask what she was doing looking through my pictures. But there was a happy sound to her voice that stopped me from being mad. "Yeah, my grandma and I go there a lot. Have you been there?"

"Yeah, my dad used to take me sometimes, before . . . well, you know."

I thought about our conversation from yesterday and nodded. "So if you don't go over on weekends, have you been seeing him at all?"

She shrugged. "He calls me, but I haven't actually seen him in a month."

"Do you want to?"

"Yeah. But I don't wanna see Kimberly, or wonderful, awesome Jake."

"Do he and your dad get along good?"

Lizzie snorted. "Oh yeah. He finally got the son he always wanted."

"He didn't tell you that?"

"No. But it's kinda obvious."

I tried hard to think of something nice to say, but I wasn't very impulsive when it came to stuff like that. "Well . . . sorry."

She dropped my phone in her lap. "Poppy, why won't you talk about your parents?" She asked the question so softly, like maybe that'd make it easier for me to answer.

My shoulders slumped. Talking about it stunk, but I realized she was truly interested and not just being nosy. "They died."

"Like in a car accident or something?"

"No, like in a bomb blast."

Her mouth turned up in a half smile, and I knew she thought I was kidding. But as the seconds ticked past, Lizzie lost her smile. "You're joking, right?"

I dug my toe into the hard-packed ground. "The short story is that my parents picked their careers over me. They left me to go teach botany in Africa for a semester, and they ended up getting killed over there. It was a terrorist type of thing."

Lizzie stared at me. Several heartbeats passed. "Seriously?"

"Seriously."

She shook her head, like she couldn't quite convince herself I meant it. "How old were you when they left?"

"Almost one."

"So you never really knew them."

I swallowed. "I have lots of pictures." But the words sounded hollow even to me.

"But you don't actually remember them, right?"

"No," I said, sounding more irritated than I meant to. "I just know what Grandma Beth's told me."

"Wow," she said.

I put a hand over my stomach to try and push back the pain. Gunner was busy sniffing a dandelion. "Come on," I said to him, "back to work." I put him in a sit and tried the stay command again. This time he lay down. Tears filled my eyes, but I knew it had more to do with Lizzie than with Gunner. I took his muzzle in my hands and looked deep into his dark eyes. "Listen up. I'm trying to help you here. You need to cooperate a little more."

"I know what might help," Lizzie said.

I blinked fast to make the tears go away. "What?"

She hopped up. "Be right back."

I watched as she trotted off toward the shelter and disappeared inside. She returned a moment later with a sandwich baggie full of dog biscuits. "I'm pretty sure he likes these," she said. "I've seen Mom toss them in his kennel."

"Hey, thanks."

Gunner seemed to understand. He pricked up his ears, and his nose started twitching. "Dream on," I told him, "you're not getting a single bite until you do what you're supposed to."

Using the biscuits as bait, I dropped the idea of teaching stay and concentrated on come instead. It worked much better. Put him in a sit, quickly back up, call him to me, and reward him with a cookie. In less than half an hour, he was coming from about twenty feet away.

Lizzie went back to the tree and didn't talk anymore, but every time I glanced her way she was watching. I thought of her interest in the cactus house, and what she'd said about her parents, and about spray-painting the federal building, and I knew there was so much more to Lizzie than just a rebellious girl with pink highlights. I felt sorry I'd been short with her. "Thanks for getting the dog biscuits," I said as I put Gunner away in his kennel. "They helped a lot."

"Sure. Are you coming tomorrow?"

"Yeah, if Marti does."

"She could always drop you off."

I shook my head. "Trey won't let me come alone. He already took my bike away for taking off by myself."

"No way. How sucky."

I laughed, because I'd never heard anybody say that before.

"So when do you get it back?"

"Good question."

"Too scared to ask, huh?"

I gave her a sheepish grin. "Pretty much, yeah." I looked through the kennel at Gunner. He met my gaze and wagged his tail. I reached a finger through the wire and touched his nose. "See you later, boy. Gotta go walk some other dogs now." I glanced at Lizzie. "Wanna come?"

She put a finger on her nose and flattened it like a pig. "Hmm. Let me consider my options. Cleaning kennels, picking up dog poop, scrubbing out water bowls . . . Sure, walking sounds okay."

That evening after supper, Marti worked on a grant application for the shelter, while I huddled on the couch, staring at a blank page on my art pad. It was warm in the house, but only my face felt warm, the rest of me was chilled. Trey would be home soon, and I had to make good on my promise to tell him the truth. But now that it was nearly time, I couldn't think of how to go about it. I was a liar. It was one of those cold, hard truths, and there was no good way to admit it. More than anything, I wanted to keep Marti from finding out I'd lied. It would be bad enough telling Trey, but I couldn't stand the idea of Marti thinking bad of me.

I toyed with the idea of going to Trey's apartment to wait for him, but I was sure he locked his door, and not so sure he'd want me there when he wasn't home anyway. I couldn't get the sour taste of fear out of my mouth no matter how many times I swallowed. Finally I set my art pad aside and stood. "Think I'll go sit outside and look at the stars for a while."

Marti glanced over with a concerned look. "Okay, honey, but stay right out there on the porch. And you might want a jacket."

"Okay," I said. I grabbed my flannel blanket off the bed and wrapped it around my shoulders. Then I slipped out the back door and dropped into one of Marti's lounge chairs. There was only a quarter moon, and the clouds played peekaboo with the stars, but the cool air felt good against my hot face. The gentle tapping of Marti's keyboard made me think about Lizzie using my phone, and I pulled it out. I thought about texting her, but I was too scared to think of what to say.

I was scrolling through my pictures of Manito Park when I heard the low rumble of Trey's Pontiac pulling up alongside the curb. My whole body filled with pins and needles. I shoved the phone back in my pocket and drew in a long, slow breath until my lungs couldn't hold anymore.

"TJ," Marti said a minute later. "I didn't know if you were going to make it home tonight."

"Yeah," Trey said, "I got roped into an incident inquiry. Man, it smells great in here. What did you girls have for dinner?"

"Turkey potpie. There's still some left if you'd like me to warm it up for you."

"No, don't get up, Mom. I'll do it. Where's Poppy?"

I was still holding my breath and starting to feel dizzy. I let it out in a controlled rush.

"Out back," Marti said, "looking at the stars, I think. She and her grandma enjoy doing that."

"Yeah? Did you two have a good day?"

"We had a lovely day," Marti said, and I could tell she was smiling. "I only wish there was some way to help her grandma. She doesn't seem to be doing very well."

"She's not," Trey said.

And their conversation made me feel like crying, because it didn't sound like either of them expected Grandma Beth to get better.

I listened to the opening and closing of the refrigerator and the clank of a plate sliding into the microwave. "Has Poppy been keeping up with her homework?" Trey asked.

"She did some a few days ago, but I don't think she has since then. The poor little thing has had an awful lot to deal with lately."

"Yeah, I know. But getting behind won't help her any."

Marti let out a heavy sigh. "That's true. I'll mention it to her again."

"It's okay," Trey said. "I'll take care of it."

He slid open the screen door and stepped out onto the deck beside me. "Hey there, Tiger."

I tucked my elbows tight to my sides. "Hey," I said, "you're really late tonight."

"I know. I'm starving." He knelt beside my chair and looked up at the sky. "So what are you seeing up there?"

"Not a whole lot, there's too much light from all the houses. But over there" — I pointed — "you can see part of Orion. In another hour or so you'll be able to see the handle of the Big Dipper."

"You're a real expert, huh?"

"No. I just know a little about the Milky Way. Grandma Beth and I have some star maps, and we take them to the park and try to figure out the different patterns."

"I saw the Northern Lights once," Trey said.

I perked up. "Really? I've only seen pictures."

"I was on Highway 95, coming home from Idaho just before midnight. It looked like white sheets dancing in the sky. Darndest thing I've ever seen. I had to pull over and watch for a few minutes."

"You were really lucky," I said. "They're not very common around here."

"Yeah, it was pretty cool." The microwave chimed, and he stood up. "But enough stargazing for now, you need to come in and do homework."

I swallowed. It was now or never. I reached for the cuff of his jacket before he could move away. "Trey," I said, "you know those surveillance photos you showed me?"

Our eyes met, and I knew I had his instant attention. "What about them?"

I let go of his jacket and dug my fingernails into my palms. "Could I maybe look at them again?"

"New ones, or the ones I already showed you?"

A nervous giggle slipped out. "Uh . . . I didn't know there were new ones."

"There's new ones every day."

"Oh . . . yeah."

His jaw set, and despite the dim glow of the porch light, I knew he saw right through me. "What's going on, Poppy?"

I'd been sure that when I really needed them to, the words would come. But they didn't. I had no idea what to say. I popped my knuckles. "Nothing. I've just been thinking more about it is all, and I think I might've seen that Frank guy after all."

"You might've, or you did?"

I swallowed. "I don't know. That's why I want to look again."

Trey ran a hand through his hair. "Don't tell me you saw him and didn't say anything."

I wanted to put a finger to my lips, to beg him to keep his voice down so Marti wouldn't hear. "I don't know. I wasn't a hundred percent sure. I was scared." The excuses flowed out my mouth, but none of them could hold water, not even to me.

"It's okay to be scared, Poppy. But this isn't some game. It's illegal to impede an investigation by withholding information."

Withholding information? It sounded so official. "I'm really sorry, Trey. I was gonna tell you. Just not right then."

176

Trey sniffed. "When, then? What if Frank kills some-one else?"

Tears filled my eyes, and my whole body went limp with shame. "I was gonna tell you," I whispered, "just as soon as my grandma came back home."

Trey was quiet for what seemed like a long time. A car rattled by the front of the house, and a tree frog croaked from somewhere nearby. I pulled my knees up to my chest so I'd have something to hold on to. I could feel the wild thumping of my heart against my leg as the seconds passed.

"You were afraid you'd get sent back to the center," Trey finally said, but his voice had lost some of its hardness.

I nodded and felt a strange sort of relief that he'd figured it out by himself. The truth sounded so selfish inside my head, I could only guess how bad it would sound out loud. And yet I had this crazy need to make him understand.

"Grandma Beth . . . she's always been there for me. We've always been there for each other. And then they separated us, and I barely got to see her, that's why I ran away that day. But here with your mom, it's not like that. Here, it's really good. But I know that once you get . . ." My voice cracked, and I struggled to get control of it again. "Once you get

Frank, then you won't need me anymore. That's the only reason I didn't tell you before."

I searched his face for any sign that he understood, that he didn't hate me. But his jaw was still set. "All right," he said. "You bought yourself a few extra days. Now it's time to step up to bat."

Chapter Eleven

MARTI took me by the hospital on our way to the shelter the next morning. I waited for her to ask what had happened with Trey the night before, but she didn't, and I was glad. I'd done what I was supposed to; I'd identified William Eugene Frank. But all it had done was make me feel a little less guilty and a lot more afraid. Afraid they'd quickly arrest him, and afraid of what would happen to me once they did.

I was still worrying over it as Marti and I walked down the hospital hallway, and I almost ran smack into Miss Austin as she came out of Grandma's room. She wore different earrings for a change — tiny silver chains with a star at the end. "How come you're here?" I blurted.

"Well, fancy meeting you two," she said. "I just had a few things to discuss with your grandmother. She'll be happy to see you." She clicked off down the hall with no further explanation.

Marti smiled. "Well, at least we know your grandma must be awake."

I stepped into the room. The purple curtain was pushed back from the bed, and Grandma Beth was turned toward us. "Hey," I said, "you're up."

She smiled at me. "Poppy," she said. She paused to draw in a deep breath as she looked at Marti. "Good . . . morning?"

"Yes, indeed," Marti said. "You're exactly right."

I hated how hard it was for Grandma Beth to talk, like even a few words were an effort. I thought of all the long conversations we'd had in the past, all the laughing we'd done, and I felt tears threaten again. I quickly forced them back with a smile. "What was Miss Austin doing here?"

"Just checking in." She patted my hand. "How's Poppy?"

I pulled up a chair and told her all about Officer Kinsley and about convincing Carol to let me work with Gunner and about Lizzie. She smoothed a finger over my hand as I chattered on, talking enough for both of us. Her fingernails were outlined in thin blue lines. I tried to remember if they'd been there before.

"So good-looking," she said with effort, when I showed her a picture of Gunner on my phone. "What a shame if he were . . . put to sleep."

"Oh, he won't be," I said. "I'll make sure."

A warm, faraway look filled her eyes, almost like she was remembering something. "You make me so proud, Poppy."

Despite how slow the words were coming out of her mouth, a warm glow spread through me, and I smiled.

Just then a nurse came into the room. She took Grandma's temperature and blood pressure and gave her more medicine, and Marti and I decided we'd better go and let her rest. But those words she'd said about being proud of me kept replaying in my head all day, just like a favorite song, and I wished Trey had been there to hear. Maybe then he'd believe that I was a good kid, and not one who went around lying to people whenever it was convenient.

That night in bed, I stared up at Marti's ceiling, and pretended it was my bedroom ceiling at home and that I could see my glow-in-the-dark stars. Grandma Beth and I had gone to see the planetarium show at Spokane Falls Community College when I was in third grade. We'd bought the star stickers from the bookstore afterward. They had faded a bit with time, but still glowed in position — Polaris centered directly over my head, Ursa Minor above, and Ursa Major off to the left. It seemed like a long time since I'd fallen asleep beneath their comforting glow. I wondered if I ever would again.

When Marti and I got to the shelter the next morning, Lizzie was waiting with a new baggie of dog treats in one hand and a tiny orange-and-white kitten in the other.

"Awwwww, where did he come from?" I asked, stroking the kitten's head. "He's adorable."

"Somebody just brought in six of them. She's the cutest, though."

"She, huh?"

The kitten looked up at Lizzie with bright, round eyes that took up half her face, and I was surprised by the charmed look on Lizzie's face. I'd never seen her look at any of the animals that way. "You don't like her or anything, do you?"

"She looks like a Garfield, doesn't she?"

I hooted. "You already named her?"

She gave me a fake scowl. "Oh, leave me alone. I only said she *looked* like a Garfield."

"She does. Maybe you should ask your mom if you can keep her." I pointed at the baggie of dog treats. "So, I'm guessing you brought these for me?"

"Actually I brought them for Gunner."

I laughed and grabbed them from her. "Funny. Are you gonna come be my babysitter again?"

"Yeah, I'll meet you out there."

"Okay, but you better keep Garfield out of sight, or Gunner might think she's a snack," I called to her as I headed off to Gunner's area.

Gunner gave a woof of joy when I came around the corner. He usually greeted me with a wagging tail, but he'd never barked like that, and it made me take in a happy breath. I opened his kennel and hugged him. "Yeah," I said, "it's great to see you, too. Come on, boy, today is the day we conquer the stay command. Are you ready?"

Gunner and I were almost through another good session when Marti stepped out the back door of the shelter. "Hey, Marti," I called, waving her over. "Come see how good Gunner's doing. He'll stay even when I take his leash off."

She stood gazing in my direction for several seconds, almost like she hadn't heard me. Then she walked slowly over to the enclosure and rested her arms on the top of the fence.

I took a close look at her. "Are you okay?"

Her mouth pinched into a crooked line, almost like she was in pain. A creeping chill ran up my arms and down my back. "What's wrong, Marti?"

Her face crumpled. "Oh, Poppy," she said, shaking her head. "Oh . . . honey."

And I knew.

An intense buzzing filled my ears, like there were a million grasshoppers inside my head. I dropped the bag of dog treats and clutched my hands over my ears. I took a few stumbling steps before my knees buckled, and the hard ground came up to meet me.

Things meshed into a strange blur after that. Gunner's wet nose poked my cheek. Lizzie and Marti helped me stand. Someone brushed dirt off the back of my pants. I don't remember any time passing, but suddenly Trey was there. And then he and Marti and I walked across the black asphalt of the hospital parking lot. There was hushed, quiet conversation behind my back, voices I recognized and others I didn't. A doctor came to talk to us and then a hospital chaplain. One of them asked if I wanted to see Grandma Beth. No, I didn't. What I wanted was to be left alone. To slink off alone and disappear into myself.

I dozed off in Trey's car on the way back to Marti's. I don't know how I got into the house, or what time it was when I finally flopped across the bed. Marti tugged off my shoes and covered me with the blankets. Then I rolled onto my stomach, put the pillow over my head, and tried to pretend that this day had never happened.

My rumbling stomach woke me the next morning. For a few peaceful seconds all I thought about was breakfast. Then everything came back, rushing my mind with misery. *Grandma Beth.* My stomach clenched into a steel fist. *Oh, Grandma Beth.* It seemed so wrong for my stomach to growl. How could I be hungry when my whole world was gone?

Miss Austin came to the house. She made me put on a clean shirt and then took me to the center to see a counselor. The counselor's name was Mrs. Green, but her office was painted in shades of blue and white.

Mrs. Green invited me to sit on a couch beside her and gave me a cup of hot lemon tea. I sipped the tea and nibbled an energy bar while she talked. She assured me that however I was feeling was perfectly normal, and that it was okay to grieve in whatever way felt natural to me. She said that some people expressed their grief inwardly and some outwardly. She had a nice, soothing voice and said things that sounded good. She asked me to think about what she'd said and said that she'd see me the next day for another session. But I couldn't do what she asked, I couldn't think about what she'd said, because the second I walked out of her office I forgot every word.

Marti tried to get me to stay out in the living room, to listen to the messages from Lizzie, or to watch TV with her. But all I wanted was to be alone so I could try and go back to sleep. Sleeping was the only thing that blocked out the despair, but I couldn't get my mind to shut down enough to let me sleep. I was in the bedroom that evening, staring through the blinds at the dim light of dusk when Trey came home.

He and Marti talked quietly in the living room for a few minutes before he came into the bedroom and flipped on the light. "Hey, Tiger."

I groaned and flung an arm across my eyes. "Turn if off! I'm trying to sleep."

"Sounds like you're awake to me."

"I said I'm *trying* to sleep."

"That's about all you've done for the last twenty-four hours. It's time to get up now."

"I don't want to."

"But it's suppertime. You need to come eat."

"I'm not hungry."

Trey grasped my arm and pulled me up onto the edge of the bed. It startled me more than hurt, but tears jumped to my eyes anyway. I rubbed my arm. "Why can't you just leave me alone, Trey?"

He sat down beside me. "The service for your grandma is tomorrow."

I squeezed my eyes shut. "No. I'm not going to any service."

"Why's that?"

"I don't want to see her . . . dead," I said, and my voice cracked on the last word.

"You don't have to see her if you don't want. She'll be in a casket."

"I don't want to go, Trey."

He rubbed his chin and stared off into the air. "Nobody can make you go, Poppy. But I'm gonna tell you something. If you don't go, it'll be one of those decisions you'll regret for the rest of your life."

I tried to make sense of his words, but my mind felt like it had gauze wrapped around it. "Why?" I finally asked.

"Because," he said gently, "it's your chance to say good-bye. That's why."

I sucked in a trembling breath. "But I don't wanna say good-bye."

Trey sighed. He interlaced his fingers and studied them. "Okay. You give it a little more thought. But for right now, you need to come eat something. Mom's really worried about you."

"I might throw up if I eat."

He stood and held out a hand to me. "Come on, come try."

I teetered on the edge of the bed and looked at his hand. "Trey?"

"Yeah?"

"Is she really gone?"

He lowered himself onto the edge of the bed again. "Afraid so, Tiger. Come 'ere." He raised his arm, and I crawled under it and held on to him as tight as I could. The tears came out of nowhere, buckets of them, and I didn't understand how I'd ever be able to say good-bye to Grandma Beth.

Chapter Twelve

GRANDMA Beth's service was held at the Lotus Garden Cemetery. There was a little building that looked like it belonged in Japan, with stone pillars and a woven lattice roof. Twelve of us stood in a semi-circle and listened to a man in a dark suit talk about what a wonderful woman Bethany Ann Parker had been.

I stood with Trey, Marti, and Miss Austin. Carol and Lizzie came, too. Our landlady, Mrs. Gilly, was there, along with two other ladies from our apartment building. The other people I didn't know. One said he'd worked with Grandma Beth as a hospice volunteer years before. The other two were care workers from the Huckleberry Home.

The casket was plain brown with a shiny coating. A thin strip of brass trim lined both sides. The lid was closed. I wondered if Grandma Beth was really in there. But I didn't want to see, because then I'd know for sure.

After the brief service came the burial. I asked Miss Austin if I could go sit in her car and wait, and she said yes. I could tell Trey didn't like the idea. He watched me the whole way over to her car. I climbed into the backseat, waited until Trey looked away, and then slipped out the other side. I didn't think too much about where to go. All I knew was that I wanted to be someplace else . . . anywhere else but here, watching them put Grandma Beth in the ground.

I started walking, and my feet instinctively took me toward Manito Park. It was a lot farther from the Lotus Garden Cemetery than I realized. But I just kept walking until my legs burned and my feet ached and the soft green lawn of the park finally came into view.

It was quiet in the cactus house with only a few visitors ambling along the dirt pathways. I breathed in the steamy air and headed for my favorite place — a wood and wrought-iron bench hidden behind the flat, giant leaves of a banana palm. Water trickled softly in the reflection pond, and there was an occasional flash of orange from a koi goldfish.

Someone had left a half-full water bottle sitting on the bench. I hesitated only a second before I twisted the top off and drank it. Then I settled against the bench, propped my head on my hand, and closed my eyes.

It was my arm slipping off the armrest that jolted me awake.

A little boy with almond-shaped eyes squinted at me through the leaves of the banana palm while the grown-ups behind him chattered in a foreign language. I reached for my cell phone to check the time, only to remember I'd left it on the backseat of Miss Austin's car. My head felt groggy, and my stomach felt like it was touching my backbone. I hadn't eaten anything since the small bowl of applesauce Marti had coaxed into me the evening before.

I stood and stretched and walked outside to look at the clock tower. Three-thirty. Grandma Beth's service had been at eleven o'clock. It seemed strange that over four hours had passed; it didn't feel like any time had gone by at all.

My feet still ached from all the walking, and I couldn't think of any place to go. I slipped over to sit in the crinkly red leaves beneath a maple tree and watched the few people strolling around. That's when I spotted Lizzie, just coming over the hill from the parking lot. She headed toward the cactus house, dressed in black skinny jeans and white sneakers. Her bright pink highlights glinted in the sun. She noticed me a few seconds before she reached the entrance, and then turned and walked over with an uncertain wave. "Hey, Poppy."

"Hey. What are you doing here?"

She shrugged. "I thought you'd be here. Are you okay? I'm really sorry about your grandma." She dropped down in the leaves beside me. "Everybody's going bonkers looking for you."

"Yeah?"

"Mom and Marti went to check your old apartment. And Trey headed to the kids' center, I think, and I don't know where after that."

"Does anybody know you're here?" I asked.

"No. I thought you probably wanted to be alone for a while. I'll leave if you want me to."

I sagged against the tree trunk. Tears filled my eyes, and I didn't bother to brush them away. "I don't know what I want. I don't know what to do."

Lizzie didn't say anything. But she reached over and let her hand rest on my arm for a few seconds, and I was glad she was there. She cleared her throat. "That's how I felt last year, after Mom and Dad divorced. It's still kind of how I feel now."

I closed my eyes. Neither of us spoke for a while.

"What did you and your grandma do when you came here?" Lizzie finally asked.

I took a shaky breath and tried to focus on her question. "Took walks and had picnics. We watched the stars."

She picked up a maple leaf and examined its vein pattern. "Dad and I used to come here on Saturday afternoons. We'd get Italian sodas and just walk around."

"You should ask him to do it again."

"I don't think he would now. Everything's different."

A heavy pressure throbbed behind my eyes, and my throat choked with tears. "Oh, Lizzie," I said. "Just *ask* him. Someday you might not be able to."

Her eyes sparked with alarm, and I knew she got my point. Dry leaves crunched as she leaned back on her elbows.

I closed my eyes again. A squirrel scolded from the branches above. The air smelled of early-fall lilies, mixed with a hint of coconut sunscreen from someone walking past. I wondered why anyone would bother with sunscreen in October. My stomach suddenly let out a really loud gurgle.

Lizzie sniffed. "Wow. That sounded like thunder." She dug in her pocket. "I've got three dollars. Want something to eat?"

I shrugged. "No, I'm okay."

"Well, I'm kinda hungry. I'll walk over to the food cart and see what they've got."

She returned a few minutes later with a bucket of popcorn. "Is this okay? It was either popcorn or slushies, and those things are so sweet they make me hurl."

I wasn't sure if I wanted to eat or not, but the buttery smell was hard to resist. I took a handful. "Popcorn's good. Thanks."

"Speaking of food, you wanna hear something weird? Gunner's not eating."

Gunner. I'd forgotten all about him. I looked at Lizzie. "He's not eating?"

"Not much anyway. He hasn't since the other day, when you found out about your grandma. Mom says he misses you."

It seemed wrong to think about anyone besides Grandma Beth right then, but I pictured Gunner sitting beside me, strong and steady enough to lean against, and a sharp longing for him filled my heart. I took another handful of popcorn. About the time the bucket was empty, the clock tower chimed four heavy bongs.

Lizzie sighed. "Guess it's time to call Mom and get busted for disappearing. What about you? You can't stay here by yourself."

"I don't know."

"Well, I won't tell her I saw you if you don't want me to."

"She'll ask why you're here."

"I can make something up. She's already convinced I'm a bad kid, so why not live up to my rep."

"She doesn't think you're a bad kid."

Lizzie snorted. "Yeah, she does."

"No, she doesn't. She wishes you'd talk to her more. She even told me that."

Surprise flickered across her face, and I could tell she wanted to believe me but wasn't sure she could. She was quiet for a minute, then she said, "So, do you want me to tell her you're here, or not?"

I thought about my decision to lie to Trey, how it hadn't turned out very good. The last thing I wanted was for Lizzie to have to lie for me. "It's okay," I said. "You can tell her I'm here. I don't wanna stay by myself anyway."

Lizzie made the call, and I listened to Carol's voice jump back and forth between relief and exasperation. Then Lizzie slipped the phone back in her pocket and rolled her eyes. "Brace yourself. The cavalry's on its way."

"Your mom?"

"And Marti."

I slowly climbed to my feet. "Guess we might as well go wait in the parking lot." I crumpled the empty popcorn bucket and looked around for a trash can.

That's when I saw him.

A man with a black baseball cap and ripped jeans stood just off the path about thirty yards away. He was partially hidden behind the arching branches of a locust tree, smoking a cigarette and watching us.

It took my weary brain a few seconds to recognize what was familiar about him. Then all my senses jumped to full alert, like somebody had thrown a bucket of cold water on me. I took a step back.

"Are you okay?" Lizzie asked.

But I didn't answer, because I wasn't sure if I was okay or not. My brain told me the man was William Eugene Frank. But was my brain playing tricks? As soon as I'd given Trey his positive ID, Frank's name had gone out all over the news. Wouldn't he be scared? Wouldn't he run? But then I remembered something Trey had said the first night we met. *Scared people do stupid things.* And I realized that, scared or not, Frank probably needed to shut me up. Maybe he'd been keeping an eye on me, waiting for a safe opportunity when nobody else was around. A strange sound came from my throat.

Lizzie stared at me. "What's the matter, Poppy?"

"Don't look around," I ordered. "Just look at me and listen."

"Don't look at what?"

"That guy in the black hat," I said, talking out of the side of my mouth, "standing in front of the pond."

She swiveled to look even though I'd told her not to. "Stop!" I hissed. "We don't want him to know we see him."

"What are you so freaked out about, Poppy? Who is he?"

"The guy I saw rob the gas station that night. His picture's up all over town."

Lizzie's mouth dropped open. Then her eyes widened with understanding. "Oh. My. God! I told you, Poppy. Didn't I tell you?"

My heart thudded in my chest and sweat beaded under my arms. "Yeah."

"What do we do?"

"We need to get the cops here before he takes off. We need to call Trey, but I don't have my phone."

She thrust her phone out to me, but I just stared at it, frozen. "I can't think . . . I can't remember his number."

"Then just call 911."

I grabbed the phone and touched the numbers with trembling fingers.

"This is 911," said a woman's voice. "What is your emergency?"

"This is Poppy P-Parker," I stuttered. "I need to get a message to Detective Trey Brannigan. He's with the —"

Lizzie gasped. "He's coming!"

The man in the black cap headed toward us, his hat pulled low over his eyes, his gait casual. I fought back the urge to run and tried to think. There were a lot of good hiding places along the trail if we ran deeper into the park. But that meant there would be a lot of good hiding places for him, too. Maybe he'd end up getting away again. Is that what I wanted?

I wasn't sure what would happen to me if they caught him. Would I have to stay at the center until I grew up? Would I get sent to live with strangers? But there was one thing I did know for sure. I wouldn't be able to live with myself if I didn't do the right thing. I'd already helped him stay free long enough. We had to lead him toward the main entrance, where the police would come. I grabbed Lizzie by the arm. "Come on, this way!"

People stared as we raced past the cactus house, across the sloping lawn of the lilac gardens and toward the parking lot.

Lizzie panted alongside me. "Where are we going, Poppy?"

"Just follow me." I cut a sharp right turn that took us beside a row of scattered cars in the parking lot. We stopped and squatted behind the safety of an SUV, our breath wheezing in our chest. "Is he coming?" I asked.

"Don't know," Lizzie said. "Can't see him."

I stole a quick look around the bumper of the SUV. It took me a minute to spot him. He walked toward us, his head swiveling back and forth, scanning the area. "I see him. He's not running. He's trying not to draw any attention. That's good."

Lizzie's eyes were huge. "Good? Are you crazy?"

A wave of nausea gushed over me, and I put a hand on my stomach.

A faint, high-pitched sound reached my ears, and I stared around before it dawned on me that the voice was coming from Lizzie's phone. The 911 operator had stayed on the line. "Poppy, are you there?" she asked. "Talk to me if you're still there."

"I'm still here," I said. "I need to get a message to Detective Trey Brannigan. He's with the Spokane Police Department. Tell him to come to Manito Park as fast as he can. The guy they're looking for is here."

"Detective Trey Brannigan," she repeated in a remarkably calm voice. "Okay, Poppy. I'm trying to reach him now. Tell me what's going on. Are you in danger?"

"Just give him the message, please," I begged. "He'll know what's going on."

I caught glimpses of the black baseball hat bobbing along in the open spaces between the trees. "Come on," I said to Lizzie. "I know where to go."

We ran hunched over, to the far side of the parking area. Then I sprinted across to the MANITO PARK sign and over to the stone arch. I knew there was a big drainage culvert below the bridge; I'd seen it countless times with Grandma Beth.

I dropped to my hands and knees and crawled inside the corrugated metal pipe with Lizzie practically on top of me. The ground inside was cold and mushy with mud. We hovered inside the pipe, our hands and knees coated with muck and our breath coming in harsh gasps.

Tears ran down Lizzie's cheeks. "What are we g-gonna do? What if he sees us?"

"It's okay," I said. "This is a good place to hide."

"But we could get trapped in here."

The high-pitched sound reached our ears again. Lizzie grasped her phone. "Hello?" she said.

"Poppy," I heard the operator say, "I've reached Detective Brannigan. I'll transfer you."

Lizzie tossed the phone to me. I waited, breathless.

"Poppy?" Trey said anxiously. "Are you there?"

I nearly wilted with relief. "Trey," I gasped, "he's here at the park."

"Frank? Has he seen you?"

"Yeah, he's following us."

"Who's us?"

"Me and Lizzie."

"Does he know where you are right now?"

"I don't know. I don't think so. We're in a drainage pipe by the stone arch in the main parking area."

"All right, listen to me, Poppy. Stay calm, and stay put. We've got officers less than two minutes away. Okay?"

My teeth chattered. "I'm really s-scared, Trey."

"I know. But you're gonna be okay. How many people are hanging around the parking lot?"

I crawled to the opening of the culvert. I saw an older couple with a golden retriever and a kid doing tricks on his skateboard. "Only a few," I said. "It's mostly just cars."

"Good. Now tell me what Frank is wearing."

I tried to think. "Ripped jeans, just like the day at the gas station. And a black cap."

"And a blue shirt," Lizzie added.

"And a blue shirt, Lizzie says."

"Okay, hold on," Trey said. I listened while he relayed the

information over the police radio in his car. I gripped the phone. "Trey, are you still there?"

"I'm right here, Tiger. Tell me if you can see Frank."

"No, no, I don't see him. . . . I don't know where he went. Should we stay here?"

"Yes!" he said. "Don't move."

Lizzie grabbed her face. "What about Mom and Marti?"

"Carol's coming, Trey. And your mom. They'll walk right into all this."

"I'll take care of it," he said. "You just stay put, hear me?"

I raked my fingers down my cheek. "Okay, but don't hang up."

"I won't."

Lizzie tilted her head. "I think I hear them."

"Who?" I yelped. "Frank?"

"No, the cops. Listen."

I picked out the first notes of approaching sirens. "We can hear sirens, Trey. The cops are coming."

"I'm right behind them," he said.

A beige Volkswagen Bug turned in off the street and cruised by in search of a parking spot. Right as the car swung into a space, William Eugene Frank appeared at the driver's door. I sucked in a breath.

"Poppy?" Trey said. "What's wrong? Talk to me."

Lizzie squeezed up beside me. I watched, stunned, as Frank jerked open the door of the Volkswagen and dragged out a young woman in a flowered sundress. She screamed as he threw her to the pavement. "He's getting away," I cried. "He just stole a lady's car."

"Describe it to me," Trey said.

"It's a Bug. A beige-colored one. He's backing it out."

"She's gonna get run over," Lizzie yelped, pointing to the young driver.

I dropped the phone and covered my ears just as the woman scrambled out of the way and cowered behind a nearby car. And then the sound of sirens grew loud, and police cars swarmed the area. The golden retriever started to bark, and the elderly couple scattered as the blacktop turned into a field of flashing lights and squealing tires.

Police surrounded the Volkswagen. The driver's door flew open, and Frank jumped out. For a second, I thought he might make a run for it. But officers swooped in, shouting orders with guns drawn. He raised his hands and dropped to his knees.

Lizzie grabbed my arm and shook me hard. "They got him," she whooped. "They got him."

I laughed. "I know. I know." And I started to shake like a quaking aspen.

Then I spotted Trey, weaving through all the chaos and cars, heading straight toward the stone arch. Lizzie and I scrambled out of the culvert, and I threw myself against him. He laughed and tightened an arm around me. "Hey, it's good to see you little mud rats. You both okay?"

Lizzie hovered a few feet away, taking big gulps of air and hugging her arms around herself. I grabbed her hand and pulled her over to me. Trey winked at her. "I hear you were the only one smart enough to know where to find Poppy."

She stared at him blankly before her eyes widened. "Oh, uh — it was just a hunch."

"Good hunch," he said.

Lizzie ducked her head, but not before I saw her grin.

Trey put out a hand to her. "Come on, your mom's about to tear her hair out."

"She is?"

"What do you think?" he said.

William Eugene Frank stood handcuffed beside a patrol car. His back was to me, and I was glad. I didn't want to see his face, and I didn't want him to see me. All I wanted was to be far away from him. Marti and Carol waited across the street from the park, eagerly staring in our direction. As soon as they caught sight of us, they both came running over. Carol threw her arms around Lizzie, laughing while tears ran down her face. "Oh, baby!" she said. "I was so worried about you."

Marti just wrapped her arms around me and rocked me back and forth like I was a little kid. "I'm so sorry for all you've had to deal with," she whispered in my ear. "So, so sorry. And even though you may not believe it right now, things will get better. You'll see."

I closed my eyes. How could things get better? Grandma Beth was gone. Nothing could ever be the same. I'd have to go back to the center — for good. But her words still calmed me. "I sure hope you're right," I whispered.

"How did you guys know what was going on?" Lizzie asked.

"TJ had an officer call us as soon as he heard from the 911 operator," Marti said.

"Worst phone call of my life," Carol added.

Lizzie stepped back and gave her mom a silly grin. "Really? Worse than the one saying I got caught spray-painting the federal building?"

"Oh my God," Carol said. "Way worse. Way, way worse." She wiped at her face. "So now that I've aged ten years in the last thirty minutes, what do I do with the rest of my evening?"

Marti laughed. She checked her watch. "Well, you know, it just happens to be dinnertime. What do you say we get these girls into some clean clothes and then go get a bite to eat?" She looked at me. "Can you eat something, Poppy?"

"I don't know," I said. "I'll try."

Lizzie smiled. "Let's do it, Mom. A big greasy hamburger and fries."

"Sounds good to me," Carol said.

I glanced around for Trey, but he was gone.

Marti seemed to read my mind. She gestured toward the parking lot. "Can't keep a detective away from the action for long. This is a big day for him."

I took a shuddering breath as I looked over at all the police cars and flashing lights across the street. And I felt proud that I'd helped to bring a criminal to justice, but mostly I just felt tired. "He can have it," I said. "I've had all the action I can take."

Chapter Thirteen

I SLEPT late the next morning and woke to the smell of bacon frying. Marti and I lingered over our omelets and orange juice and watched some morning news show. We didn't talk about the phone call Trey had warned us to expect — the one from Miss Austin, saying it was time for me to go back to the center. I prayed that just maybe there would be a miracle, that she wouldn't call, that maybe she'd forget I existed.

But there was no miracle. The call came early that afternoon, when I was curled up on the couch, finishing a sketch of Harvey and trying not to think about Grandma Beth. The sound of the phone made my muscles cramp, and I bumped the volume down on the TV. I could tell it was Miss Austin from the hesitant way Marti spoke. "Yes, he was arrested last night. Yes, that's right. Well, yes it's good news . . . certainly."

After the phone call she came into the living room and sat beside me. I sighed. "Will I still get to see you?"

"Of course you will. You want to keep going to the shelter with me, don't you?"

I perked up a little. "Can I do that?"

"Absolutely. Miss Austin knows you're training Gunner. And I don't see why we can't do other things together as well. Would you like that?"

I bit the inside of my lip and looked down at my sketch of Harvey. "You know," I said, "when Trey first brought me here, I couldn't figure out why. I thought it was so weird. But now, I don't know how I would've got through everything without you, Marti."

She scooted close and turned my chin toward her. "You listen to me, Poppy, because I've got news for you. You're not through with me yet. Not by a long shot. Got that?"

"Okay," I whispered. And both of us started to cry.

Trey came to get me an hour later. We didn't talk on the drive over. I felt more numb than anything, at least until Trey inched through the center's main gate and parked near the front entrance. Then it all started to feel sickeningly real. We both climbed out of the car and stood for an awkward moment. I started counting the spokes on the front passenger wheel. I got to sixteen before Trey cleared his throat.

"We owe you a lot, Poppy. You deserve credit for breaking this case. I'm proud of you."

I nodded. I knew if I opened my mouth, I'd start bawling.

Trey pulled a business card from his wallet and handed it to me. "Keep this, it's the number I can be reached at anytime. My cell phone is the one on the bottom. If you need anything, call me. Okay?"

I nodded again and shoved the card in my pocket.

Trey pulled me to him and gave me a tight squeeze.

I wanted to hug him back, to bury my head against his shirt and beg him not to leave me. But I knew I didn't have the right.

"See you, Tiger. Keep your chin up, you hear? I'll be checking on you."

I turned and headed for the double glass doors. I wanted to wave as he drove off. But I gritted my teeth and didn't look back.

Right as I reached to open the door, a woman pushed through, leading a smiling little girl by the hand. I couldn't remember her name, but I knew it was the little girl who cried all the time. She wore bright red overalls, and her hair was done up in braids. She didn't act like she recognized me. The woman held the door for me. "Go ahead, hon."

"Thanks," I mumbled.

Miss Austin waited inside. She told me I had another appointment to see the grief counselor the next day and then pointed me toward my old room.

"That little girl who just left," I said. "What's her name again?"

"Erin."

"Right, Erin. Who was that with her?"

"Her mother. She and her husband were able to work things out."

"Oh," I said as an odd mix of gladness and envy rushed through me. "A happy ending."

"The best kind," Miss Austin said.

I plodded down the hall and paused in the doorway to the room. I looked at the small window with its dirty white shade rolled up to the top, and at Sidney's bed — unmade as usual, surrounded by clothes and Skittles wrappers. A pair of her jeans lay on top, bright pink underwear poking out. A shudder of fear passed over me. I still didn't know the whole story of how Trey had gotten my cell phone back from her. She'd probably hate me even more than she did before.

My bed had been stripped down to the mattress with sheets and blankets folded neatly — waiting for me. I didn't have a pillow, but Sidney had two, so I took one of hers. I flopped on the bed and stared up at the dingy ceiling. I couldn't quit thinking about that little girl, Erin. It was crazy to be jealous of a four-year-old who'd gotten her family back. I should've been happy for her, but my stomach burned instead. There was just something so unfair about the whole situation.

A long cobweb floated from the light fixture, swaying in the air currents. I hated cobwebs. They gave me the creeps. I dug in my bag for a pair of socks and tossed them at the cobweb. It danced wildly, taunting me for missing. I threw a wadded-up T-shirt and missed again. Sudden hot rage surged through me. I yanked off my left tennis shoe and hurled it. The plastic light fixture flew off with a sharp *pop*, and the bulb burst into pieces. Hot slivers rained down.

"Jeez!" I yelped, stunned.

All I could think of was getting the broken glass picked up before anyone saw what I'd done. I gathered up the bottom of my shirt and raced around the room, scooping up shards of broken glass. Then I slunk down the hall to the bathroom and dumped the whole mess in the trash can.

The little finger on my right hand throbbed. Blood seeped from a small gash, and the sight of it sent a new panic through me. Finally I rinsed my finger, wrapped it with several layers of toilet paper, and tucked it in as best I could.

My finger still throbbed an hour later when everyone came back after school. Sidney stalked into the room, and a flicker of surprise crossed her ugly face. "You're back."

"Not by choice," I said.

She dropped her backpack and sweatshirt on the floor. "Hey, what happened to my other pillow?"

"I thought . . . one was mine."

"Well, you thought wrong. Go bum one off somebody else." She strode over and yanked the pillow from my bed. "And don't touch anything else of mine or I'll break your face, got it?"

I slipped into the crowded hallway and out the back door, to where the building's walls met at an odd angle and created a little hideaway. I crawled inside and leaned against the cold cement. It was a lot like hiding in the culvert but without the mud. I could see part of the grove of aspen trees across the street. Grandma Beth called them dancing trees, because of the way their leaves shimmered and shook in the slightest breeze. *Grandma Beth.*

212

I wrapped my fingers around the card from Trey and started to cry. I wished I'd waved good-bye to him. I closed my eyes. I'd hated the center even before I met Trey or Marti, but now it felt like death row. I knew if I stayed, I'd be smothered. Maybe I'd run away. I didn't have any money, but there was still several hundred dollars in the envelope Grandma Beth kept at home. It would be enough to get me someplace warm where I could live outside, and then I wouldn't need much money. Maybe California. California was warm. It probably had oranges and grapefruit and mangos year-round. It had Disneyland, too. Grandma Beth had always talked about taking me someday.

The more I thought about it, the faster my heart started to pound. There was still food at home. I could pack enough for a week or so and then try to get a ride. I wondered how many miles it was to California. Probably at least a thousand.

But then from someplace across the street a dog barked, and it made me startle. *Gunner!* How could I just run off and abandon Gunner? I saw his dark, trusting eyes and felt him leaning into me. What would happen if I stopped working with him? He'd never qualify for police training. And I heard Grandma Beth's voice, just as clear as the day I'd stood beside her hospital bed. *You make me so proud . . . You make me so proud*. And it made me cry all the harder, because I knew if I ran away, I wouldn't just be letting Gunner down, I'd be letting her down, too. I leaned my head against the concrete and wondered why doing the right thing always seemed so hard.

That night I slept without a pillow. The next day I went to school, but I kept to myself and didn't really talk much to anyone. Luke said hi to me and asked where I'd been. But I didn't know how to answer him. I didn't know where to even start. So I just asked a question about his latest drawing — a strange-looking space creature with a square head and scaly skin. He answered my question, but after that he mostly shied away, like he realized something big had changed in the time I'd been gone.

I spent most of my time in class staring out the window and longing for Grandma Beth and Marti and Trey. I could smell Grandma's rose hand lotion and Trey's jacket, and I could feel Marti's arms around me. I missed them all so much it made my head throb.

I called Marti that evening. She sounded so happy to hear from me. She promised to work things out with Miss Austin so she could take me to the shelter.

The next day I didn't bother with school. I spent most of

it in my concrete hideaway texting with Lizzie and sketching Gunner in different poses. About the time everyone got back that afternoon, I blended into the crowd and slipped inside to my room. My whole body ached from sitting on concrete, and my cut pinkie still hurt. I knew I should probably put some clean toilet paper around it, but when I tried to unwrap the old paper, it stuck to the cut. I sat on the bed, trying to decide what to do, when I heard footsteps behind me. I turned, dreading Sidney. My mouth dropped open when I saw it was Trey.

I jumped up. "Oh, hey, you did come to see me."

His mouth turned up at one corner. "Hey, yourself. Are you sick?"

"No. Do I look sick?"

"How come you weren't in school?"

The hair on the back of my neck prickled, and I started to laugh. "What makes you think I wasn't?"

"That's a classic sign of deception, you know, when a suspect answers a question with a question."

"I didn't know I was a suspect," I said. But he didn't smile like I'd hoped.

"Why weren't you in school, Poppy?"

I dropped down on the bed again. "I dunno."

He came and sat beside me, and it made the mattress slope down. He leaned forward and rested his elbows on his knees. I breathed in the damp, earthy smell of his jacket, and even though I knew he wasn't very happy with me, I had to fight the urge to lay my head on his shoulder.

"What happened to your finger?" he asked.

"I cut it."

"Don't they have Band-Aids in this place?"

"Probably. I never asked."

He lifted my hand for a closer look. "You know, when it bleeds through like this you need to change it."

"I just tried a few minutes ago, but it's stuck to my cut."

"That's why you shouldn't use toilet paper." He pulled his wallet from his back pocket and took out a bandage. "I always keep a couple in here. Let me see your hand again."

I reluctantly held out my finger, and he unwrapped it.

The cut had turned into an angry red welt. Just looking at it made me wince. "This is a good cut," he said. "How did you get it?"

"I — it's just a bad paper cut."

He opened a small pocket knife attached to his key ring and carefully sawed away the toilet paper right up to the cut. I gritted my teeth and tried not to whimper.

"This is way too deep for a paper cut. My guess would be glass." He tore open the Band-Aid and wrapped it around my finger. "So are you gonna tell me?"

Heat warmed my face. "Okay, fine. I threw my shoe at the stupid light fixture and it broke."

Trey looked up at the ceiling. He didn't say anything for what felt like forever. I didn't realize I'd been holding my breath until I started feeling light-headed.

"What were you so upset about?"

"About being here."

"So, is that what your grandma would want? To hear about you skipping school, messing around?"

My nose filled with the sharp sting that comes right before you start to cry. I gave an exaggerated shrug. "I don't know, Trey. I just don't care about school anymore."

"No?" He reached behind me and picked up my drawing pad. He flipped through the four sketches of Gunner I'd drawn earlier. "This looks like the dog at the shelter. Gunner, right? You still care about him?"

I sniffled. "Yeah."

"That's what I thought. So here's some motivation. No school, no animal shelter."

I caught my breath. "But your mom promised to take me

as soon as she works things out with Miss Austin. I'm training him."

"Well, maybe you should've thought about that before you skipped school."

I searched his face, sure he couldn't mean it. "You don't understand, Trey. I have to go to the shelter with your mom. She and Lizzie are the only ones I have left. Everybody else left me."

"Your grandma didn't leave you, Poppy — she died. Big difference. Your parents didn't leave you, either. They were killed."

I gaped at him. "They did, too, leave me. It was their choice."

Trey sniffed. "You're telling me they went to Botswana with the express purpose of getting killed so they wouldn't have to raise you?"

All I could do was stare at him.

"What?" he said. "That's how you make it sound."

"But they made the decision to go," I said. "They could've stayed with me."

He shook his head. "You know, Poppy, I don't know much about botany, but I bet your parents put a whole lot of work and expense into earning their degrees. The chance to teach at a foreign university was probably like a dream reward. You really think it was wrong for them to go? They were victims, just like the cashier at the gas station. You think it was wrong of her to go to work the morning she got shot?"

I gritted my teeth. "It's not the same thing. That was her job."

"And your parents' job was . . . what?"

I didn't want to cry in front of him again, but my bottom lip started to shake and I couldn't help it. "To raise me," I said. "Their job was to raise me."

Trey put his arm around me, and I fell against him. "Okay," he said. "You're right. All I meant is, we're all faced with choices, and as bad as we might want to, we can't always control the outcome. Some choices turn out in ways you never saw coming, and you get blindsided, you know? They change things forever." He let out a long, slow breath. "Now I know you've had to deal with some tough stuff. Life stinks. But trying to cope by getting yourself in trouble is counter-productive. It's like an alcoholic trying to cope by taking another drink. Know what I'm saying?"

I looked down at the floor. I wasn't a hundred percent sure what *counterproductive* meant. But I *did* understand

Grandma Beth would be furious with me if she knew how I'd been acting. "Okay," I whispered. "I'll try to do better, Trey. I'll go to school. But I really need to go to the shelter with your mom."

He gave me a squeeze. "Fair enough," he said.

Chapter Fourteen

TWO weeks limped past. Marti got permission to take me to the shelter each Wednesday and Friday after school, plus Saturday mornings. School forced my mind onto other things and working at the shelter with Lizzie and Gunner gave me something to look forward to, but I still missed Grandma Beth every minute of every day. Nights were the worst. I'd scrunch down under the privacy of my flannel blanket and text Lizzie when I couldn't sleep. She always answered, so I guess she had a hard time falling asleep, too.

Our scary day at Manito Park had knocked down whatever wall was left between us, and it became a lot easier to share stuff with each other. I told her about Sidney, how she snored at night, and how hard it was to share a room with somebody you were scared of. I told her about the history test I'd failed because I didn't study, and how I worried

Gunner might not be trained good enough to pass his test with Officer Kinsley.

She admitted that I was a better friend to her than Brett had ever been. She told me she was afraid to be nice to Kimberly or Jake, because it might make her dad think she was okay with the divorce — which she wasn't. And she admitted that when people came to the shelter to look at kittens, she kept Garfield hidden.

Usually after an hour or so of texting, Lizzie and I would finally get sleepy, and I'd tuck the phone under my pillow and be able to rest.

My nerves were all jittery the morning Officer Kinsley came back to check on Gunner's progress. I waited with Gunner in his kennel, quietly stroking his head until I saw the patrol car drive up, then I took his muzzle in both hands and studied his trusting eyes. "This is it, boy. This is your chance to prove what a great dog you are. But it's for me, too, and for Grandma Beth. It's for all three of us, okay?" I kissed him on the nose. "Let's do it, boy. Let's go do it!"

Officer Kinsley and Carol waited near the enclosure as I brought Gunner out on his leash. Marti and Lizzie watched from the back door of the shelter. Lizzie gave me a thumbs-up.

I ordered Gunner into a sit position and he dropped neatly to his haunches. I raised the leash and gave it a crisp tug. "Come, boy." I trotted around the enclosure, with Gunner at my side, his shoulder brushing my leg, just like Carol's dog-training book said it should. Then I put him back in a sit, stood directly in front of him, and pointed my finger at his forehead. "Stay," I said.

I dropped his leash, not quite sure what to expect since this was the command we'd worked on the least. I stepped back several feet, keeping my finger pointed at him, pleading with him not to move. His big brown eyes fixed on me, waiting for any small sign from me to release him, but he stayed put. I walked in a 360-degree circle around him. Then I glanced at Officer Kinsley.

He clapped his approval. "Good, now let's see how he does with me." He walked over and patted Gunner's head. He gently raised his lips to check his teeth and ran his hands over his ribs. Gunner gave me a puzzled look when I handed over the leash, but as soon as Officer Kinsley said, "Gunner, come," he obediently fell into step. They circled the enclosure three times before coming to a stop near us.

"I'll tell you what," Officer Kinsley said. "I think he's got some real potential. I don't see any reason why we can't try him at the next level of training. Let me check the schedule, and I'll get back with you." He pumped my hand. "Great job, maybe a few years down the road we could use you at the academy."

Carol squealed, and I couldn't help but laugh. It was the proudest moment of my life. I remembered Trey's story, about how he'd beaten his dad at checkers on his thirteenth birthday, and I understood.

Carol waited until the patrol car pulled away from the shelter before she started jumping around like a little kid. She grabbed my shoulders and gave me a shake. "You did it!" she cried. "Way to go, girl. I can't believe you."

Marti came over and hugged me, and Lizzie gave me a high five.

It would've been a perfect moment, if only Grandma Beth could've been there to see it. And the fact that she wasn't was like a kick to the stomach. It was the first *happy* thing Grandma Beth had ever missed. She'd always been there to help me celebrate — my win in the junior art contest, my perfect-attendance award in second grade, my starring role in *Little Red Riding Hood*, my fifth-grade graduation.

And later that night, when I was alone, I cried not only because Grandma had missed my exciting day, but for

Gunner, too. Because as badly as I wanted him to move on to the next stage of training, I didn't want to let him go. He'd been like my security blanket these past several weeks, and now he'd be leaving me, too. And it made me think of my conversation with Trey about my parents' decision to go to Botswana.

Grandma Beth had told me they'd struggled to make up their minds, that they'd spent a lot of time talking it over with her. But I'd never really believed her, never *wanted* to believe her. It felt safer and easier just to blame them. But now I knew Trey was right. They hadn't *planned* to abandon me. All they'd wanted was to realize a dream. If they'd taught for the semester and then come home, it wouldn't have affected my life at all. They didn't have any more control over the way things turned out than I did over Grandma Beth dying. Sometimes things just happened. It was another one of those cold, hard-as-steel truths.

I tugged my flannel blanket up to my chin. And for the first time, I felt my resentment start to loosen.

Miss Austin came to my room the next day after school. She wore a flowing green skirt that actually looked nice on her. "Hey there, Poppy," she said. "I need you to come along with me to an appointment."

I closed my sketch pad and rolled up from the bed. "What appointment?"

"The lawyer's finished looking over your grandma's will, and he'd like to talk with you about it."

I knew Grandma Beth had a will, but I'd never asked her anything about it. All adults had wills, didn't they? "Why does he need me?"

"He has some things to tell you. He'll explain when you get there. It shouldn't take long. Bring your art pad if you like."

I followed Miss Austin to her car, and we rode downtown to a building that said SMITH & HURLEY — ASSOCIATES AT LAW. I could've drawn while we waited, but Miss Austin and I sat in red leather chairs only inches apart, and I didn't like people watching me work. I studied the artwork on the walls instead, wondering why I felt nervous. I was sure Grandma Beth had left everything in the apartment to me — she didn't have anyone else to leave it to. There were only a few things I really wanted. Grandma's photo albums and her big cactus and our book of quotations, for sure. But would there be a safe place to keep them at the center? And what about everything else? Our furniture and beds, and my books and toys?

I was about to ask Miss Austin about it when a short,

balding man came into the room. He introduced himself as Franklin Hurley and showed us into his office.

He rolled two chairs up to his black metal desk. "Have a seat, ladies. Sorry to have kept you waiting."

He opened a file folder and took out a sheet of paper along with a business-size envelope. "I assume you're Priscilla Marie Parker?"

"Poppy," I said.

"All right, Poppy. Your grandmother had a standard will, giving you the right to anything of value, including her jewelry and personal effects, as well as a bank account containing $16,342."

That caught my attention. "Sixteen thousand?"

"Yes, but you won't have access to the money right now. It will remain in a trust fund until you turn eighteen." He paused long enough to fold his hands. "Of course, your grandma was most concerned with your welfare in the event of her death, and a few weeks ago she wrote some instructions with the help of Miss Austin here." He held out the envelope. "I'll excuse myself for a few minutes and give you a chance to read it over."

I stared at the envelope before slowly reaching out and taking it. Instructions about my welfare? What was that supposed to mean? I glanced at Miss Austin and then back at the envelope. The flap was open. I slowly took out the letter and unfolded it. I felt a pang in my heart when I thought about the effort it would have taken Grandma Beth to write me a letter.

My dearest Poppy,

You've been nothing but a joy to me over the years, and I thank you so much for enriching my life in a million different ways. I regret that I can't be with you now, but I have complete faith and confidence in your ability to make a success of yourself. I love you so much.

Tears jumped to my eyes, and I had to squeeze them hard for a minute before I could keep reading. Miss Austin held out a tissue, and I grabbed it from her.

Marti Brannigan and I have had many opportunities to speak over these past days, and I have come to regard her as a dear friend. I feel blessed that you came into contact with her and her son, and I have no doubt they have your best interests at heart. I can't stand the thought of you spending the rest of your childhood at the center, or worse yet, with strangers in foster care, and the Brannigans agreed. So I've arranged to sign over custody of you to Trey, who has offered to take over legal guardianship.

I sucked in a breath. I knew I'd read the words right, but still. . . . I reread the last sentence to see if it still said the same thing. It did.

I know that no one could ever love you as much as your parents and me. But I feel in my heart that this is the best decision. I hope you understand and accept it, and that you do your very best to make your new circumstances work. I have no doubt that you will.

I sagged back in the chair as a strange heat tingled through my chest.

Miss Austin raised her eyebrows. "Did you finish?" she asked gently.

I looked back at the letter. There was still a paragraph left.

Now I want to ask just one final favor of you, Poppy. When things are tough, look up to the stars and remember all those wonderful times we looked at them together, and know that I'll love you for as long as they shine. Right now it may seem

that all the world has changed, but if you're strong, and take
one day at a time, I promise that things will fall into place.

All my love,
Grandma Beth

I dropped the letter in my lap and covered my face with my hands, too scared to accept what I'd just read. A light pressure on my shoulder made me look up a minute later. "Well?" Miss Austin asked with a smile.

I took the tissue and blew my nose. "Do you know what the letter says?"

"I do. I was there when it was notarized. What do you think?"

My mind felt thick and foggy. I raised my hands and then let them drop. "I don't know," I said.

"What's not to know?"

I started to laugh, an uncontrollable giggle that made it hard to talk. "Who would I actually live with?"

"Trey would be your legal guardian. That means he'd be responsible for you. But I think you'd get to spend a lot of time with Marti, which was what your grandma was banking on."

I took a deep breath and tried to stop laughing. "I thought Marti didn't want to take in any more foster kids."

"You're not a foster child, Poppy. You were just temporarily in the care of the state, since your grandma couldn't take care of you. But she had the legal right to assign someone of her choice as your legal guardian. In fact, once we have a brief hearing before a judge and it becomes official, you won't have to bother with me ever again."

I fingered the letter and made Miss Austin wait while I reread it. "My grandma's still trying to take care of me, isn't she?"

"Yes," Miss Austin said, "of course she is."

"Marti and Trey have already agreed to this?"

"Marti was more than willing to become your legal guardian. But after we all talked it over, she agreed that in view of her age, it might be the wisest course to make Trey the guardian."

"So . . . he just got dragged into the deal?"

She chuckled. "Well, I'm not claiming to know Detective Brannigan that well. But from what I do know, I can't quite picture him being dragged into anything. Can you?"

I thought about it and another grin slipped out. "No," I said, "not really."

She winked at me. "I'm going to tell Mr. Hurley we're ready to finish up here."

The lawyer came back in. I sat in a daze and listened to him explain that it would take several weeks until we'd have the hearing before a judge, but that Child Services had agreed there wasn't any reason I couldn't stay with Trey and Marti in the meantime.

Marti was waiting for us in the lobby. She jumped up, and the magazine she'd been reading fell off her lap. She clenched her hands, looking like she was afraid maybe things hadn't gone well. But then Miss Austin said, "Congratulations," and Marti's face relaxed into a big grin.

She came over and put her fingertips on my cheek. "So what do you think? Are you willing to consider living with an old lady and her bossy son?"

"Why didn't you tell me, Marti?"

"She didn't tell you," Miss Austin answered, "because I asked her not to. There was too much chance of disappointing you if things didn't pan out." She gave my shoulder a pat and looked at Marti. "Why don't you follow me back to the center. I'll need you to fill out some paperwork, and then Poppy can get her things."

I followed Marti out to her car, clutching Grandma Beth's letter in my hand. I wondered if this past hour had really happened, or if it was some weird dream. But then I slipped into the front seat and reached out to touch the little vanilla-scented tree dangling from Marti's radio, and I knew it was real. Unbelievable, but real.

Trey worked late again that night, but once he got home he called me over to his half of the duplex. "Can we sit out on the steps?" I asked. "The stars are out."

He brought out a beer and a couple of Twinkies, and sat beside me on the cold cement. We looked up at the night sky, but neither of us spoke. I wondered what he was thinking. I was thinking how good it felt to be sitting beside him again.

"So, there's gonna be chores," he said, "and rules."

"Yeah? Like what?"

"No skipping school, that's for sure. And no pink hair, either."

I giggled. "Lizzie offered to give me some sun streaks. Would that be okay?"

"Sun streaks?"

"Yeah, you know, like lighter highlights."

Trey furrowed his brow like he didn't know what to say, and I giggled again. "Any more rules?"

"No more than two Twinkies a week."

"What!" I gasped. "Oh, man. You saved the worst for last."

"Yeah, well, there'll be more once I've had a chance to think. You have any questions?"

"Yeah. Can I have my bike back now?"

"Yep. But no taking off without permission."

"Okay." I let out a slow, even breath. "I just have one more question. Why did you agree to this, Trey?"

He gave the beer bottle a thoughtful look and rubbed his thumb over its top. "Because once I had a chance to help a really great kid, and I didn't. And I try never to make the same mistake twice."

"Virginia?"

"She used to be my next-door neighbor. I guess I told you that. Sweet little kid. She had these big eyes like yours. Sometimes she'd see me outside and come over to talk."

He smiled sadly, but not at me.

"She had this hamster named Ralph. She was convinced the little rodent could do everything but talk. She'd help me wash the car or clean up the garage and tell me all about Ralph."

I stayed completely still, afraid the slightest movement might break the spell and make him stop talking.

"Her folks worked late most nights, left the older step-brother to babysit. He picked on her a lot. One night I heard Virginia crying, and I went over to find out what was going on. Her brother had sprained her wrist because she wouldn't listen to him. I called the parents and told them they better get home because I was gonna arrest their son for assault. But the mom, she started to cry, gave me some song and dance about what a rough time the family had been going through and begged me to let them handle it on their own."

Trey waved his hand in disgust and glanced at me. "I agreed to give him one more chance. Can you believe it? I actually agreed. Worst decision I've ever made."

I gave a slight nod.

"Things were okay for a couple weeks," he said. "I saw Virginia several times and she seemed good. Then one night — a Friday night — the brother invited a bunch of his buddies over to get high and . . . and then . . ."

He stopped. His hands curled into fists. "Nobody's sure exactly what happened then. She probably threatened to tattle and her brother freaked out. All I know is we had a dead little girl, five teenage boys, and five different stories. The whole department put their all into that case, but there was never enough hard evidence to prove who'd done what. The case went to trial, but nobody was ever convicted."

He shook his head. "God, how I wish I'd followed my gut and arrested the kid that first night."

I looked down at my shoes as a shiver passed through me. It creeped me out a little to know that I reminded him of a dead girl. But I was really touched that he trusted me enough to tell me the story. I wondered what had happened to the little hamster, Ralph. "You know," I said, "her brother might have still hurt her later."

"Maybe."

"Well," I said, "I guess it's like you told me not long ago — some choices turn out good, and some . . . blindside you."

"Yeah."

The glowing half moon slowly rose until it peeked its way above the house across the street. It cast a soft shine on the pavement. Soon after, the chirping of a lone cricket filled the air.

"Well," Trey said, "guess he thinks it's officially nighttime."

"Guess he does."

"That means you better head for bed."

"Okay." I stood and stretched and looked up at the sky once more. "Will you go with me to Manito Park sometime? The stars are so much brighter there."

"Sure," he said. Then he reached for my hand and gave it a firm shake. "Welcome to the Brannigan family, Tiger."

I was too overcome to say anything. I think he understood.

He took another sip of beer and then said, "Go on now. Good night."

Marti and I spent the next morning at the shelter. I let Gunner run around in the fenced area while Lizzie and I cleaned up dog poop and laughed at Garfield's efforts to box with a dandelion.

"I'm taking him with me tomorrow," Lizzie said.

"Home you mean?"

She puffed out a sigh and shook her head. "No, I'm going to visit Dad tomorrow."

I sucked in a breath. "Really? Good for you."

"Yeah, well, we'll see. But I figure Garfield will give us something to talk about. I'm not sure what else we'll do."

"You could always go for a walk through Manito Park."

She made big eyes. "Not so sure I'm ready to go back there yet. So what do you think will happen to him?"

"Who?"

"William Eugene Frank."

"Oh." I shook my head. "Trey says he'll stay in prison until his trial, which probably won't be till next year. And then he should get sent away for a long time after that."

"I hope so. Hey, speaking of next year, guess what?"

"You'll be a year older?"

"Funny. No, Mom says if I finish my community service and promise to stay out of trouble, she might let me go back to middle school."

I grinned. "To Whitmore? We'd be together."

"I know. How cool is that?"

"As cool as ice cream in November," Marti said.

And both of us whirled around to see that she'd come up behind us. "I'm serious," she said. "I think we need to take a lunch break and go celebrate."

"Really?" I said. "Ice cream for lunch?"

"Why not?" Marti said.

Lizzie let her shovel clang to the ground and scooped up Garfield before making a beeline for the gate. "Only an idiot would turn that down. Race you to the car, Poppy."

"Hold up there," Marti called. "In view of what you girls were just doing, don't you think you should wash your hands first?"

It was after I'd dried my hands and reached into my pocket for my ChapStick that I felt Grandma Beth's letter. I'd kept it with me ever since the other day in the lawyer's office, and it was already worn soft from all the folding and unfolding. I knew if I didn't put it in a safe place soon, it would end up falling apart. But I wasn't quite ready to put it away. There was something I needed to do first, and as Marti and Lizzie and I headed across town, I knew it was time.

"Marti," I asked, "could we make a quick stop by the cemetery before we go for ice cream?"

She met my eyes with a warm smile. "Of course we can," she said.

I took Grandma Beth's letter out of my pocket and read it again, until the car slowed and we came to a stop. I looked out my window. Across the street, a tall white church hovered, its steeple reaching for the sky. Spread out behind it was a huge green lawn, surrounded by a wrought-iron fence. "Where's the little Japanese building?" I asked.

"I brought you to the back side. It's closer to where your Grandma's buried."

"Where is she?"

"One row to the left of the center, about a third of the way down. I can show you. Or you could take Lizzie."

"Is it okay if I go alone?" I half expected her to say no — it had been a long time since I'd been allowed to do anything by myself.

But she said, "We'll wait right here."

Lizzie wiggled her eyebrows at me. "Don't take too long. I'm hungry."

I climbed out of the car and slipped through the open

gate, veering left like Marti had said. I glanced at each gravesite until I found the still-fresh mound of dirt and the marker that read BETHANY ANN PARKER. It was a small black stone, set flat on the ground and dwarfed by a big bouquet of white daisies and red poppies. The dirt was damp from the sprinklers. It smelled like Trey's jacket.

I sunk down on my knees beside the marker and traced Grandma Beth's name with my fingertip. I didn't feel like crying at all. I felt almost happy, peaceful, glad to see her in such a beautiful place. "I'm sorry I didn't come to the burial," I said. "I hope you're not mad at me. I love you, Grandma Beth."

I sat there for ten minutes, letting handfuls of dirt sift through my fingers while the cool breeze played with my hair and the light perfume of roses drifted across from the next row. I thought about all the good times with Grandma Beth — all the cookies we'd baked, the constellations we'd studied, the hugs, and the love. And it was so hard to think about a future without her. But then I looked down at her letter again, and I realized, I didn't have to think a long way into the future. All I had to do was think about the next day.

"One day at a time," I whispered. I carefully worked a poppy free of the bouquet and cradled it in my hand as I walked back to the car.

"About time," Lizzie teased. "We were gonna leave you."

Marti shook her head and gave me an apologetic look, like she was sorry I had to endure Lizzie. But I just smiled. I liked Lizzie's off-the-wall comments. They had a way of making things seem not so bad.

"So," Marti said as we pulled back onto the road, "I think this should be a two-scoop celebration. What flavor is everyone in the mood for?"

"Chocolate and chocolate," Lizzie piped up, before I even had a chance to think.

I gave her a weird look. "Why would you get both scoops the same?"

Lizzie gave a long-suffering sigh. "Ice cream should only come in two flavors. Chocolate for the smart, cool people, and vanilla for the really boring types who don't know any better."

Even Marti cracked up at that one. "Well . . . I've never heard *that* take on the subject before."

Lizzie gave me a sad look. "Let me guess, with you back to being a G-rated person, your favorite is probably vanilla."

"G-rated?" Marti asked.

"Just ignore her," I said. "She's on the road to self-destruction."

Marti looked truly speechless after that one, and both Lizzie and I burst out laughing.

"But I'm right, huh?" Lizzie asked. "You want vanilla."

"No, you're not right," I said. "You're totally wrong, as usual. I happen to like lots of flavors — strawberry, rocky road, caramel, butter pecan . . ."

Lizzie groaned. "Well, all I can say is you better have it figured out by the time we get there. I'm not waiting a half hour for you to decide."

"Maybe," I said, and gave her a smug look just to bug her.

But the truth was, I wouldn't need any time to decide. I already knew exactly what I wanted — a big scoop of butter pecan for Grandma Beth, and a scoop of Moose Tracks for me.

Because that was my favorite.

Acknowledgments

I'VE always loved dogs. And most of the dogs that have graced my life have come from local animal shelters. A huge thank-you to all those shelter employees who bring a little sunshine into the lives of all the deserving pets waiting for homes.

A big thank-you to my editor, Jody Corbett, who understood from the beginning what I was trying to say with this story, and whose skillful direction raised it to new heights. Thanks also to the rest of the hardworking folks at Scholastic, many who toil behind the scenes and never get to see their name on any page.

A special thanks to my supremely supportive agent, Lara Perkins, who amazes me with her wonderful mix of cheerfulness and savvy business sense.

Heartfelt gratitude to my parents, who always told me I would succeed as a writer if I didn't give up.

And last but not least, thanks to Mary Cronk Farrell, who took the time to drive to Manito Park and confirm the exact words on the entrance sign.

About the Author

DIANNA DORISI WINGET writes fiction and non-fiction for young readers. Her first novel is *A Smidgen of Sky*. She lives in the mountains of north Idaho with her husband, their daughter, and two dogs. For more about her, visit www.diannawinget.com.